THE WORLDS
SMALLEST UNICORN
AND OTHER STORIES

Shena Mackay was born in Edinburgh. She is the author of two novellas, three collections of short stories and seven novels. Her novel *Dunedin* and the collection of short stories, *The Laughing Academy*, both won Scottish Arts Council Book Awards and the bestselling *The Orchard on Fire* was shortlisted for the 1996 Booker Prize and the McVitie's Prize. Her latest novel, *The Artist's Widow*, was published in 1998. Shena Mackay lives in London.

ALSO BY SHENA MACKAY

Shena Mackay

THE WORLDS SMALLEST UNICORN

and other stories

V

VINTAGE

Published by Vintage 2000

2 4 6 8 10 9 7 5 3 1

Copyright © Shena Mackay 1999

First published in Great Britain by
Jonathan Cape in 1999

Vintage
Random House, 20 Vauxhall Bridge Road,
London SW1V 2SA

Random House Australia (Pty) Limited
20 Alfred Street, Milsons Point, Sydney
New South Wales 2061, Australia

Random House New Zealand Limited
18 Poland Road, Glenfield,
Auckland 10, New Zealand

Random House (Pty) Limited
Endulini, 5A Jubilee Road, Parktown 2193,
South Africa

The Random House Group Limited Reg. No. 954009
www.randomhouse.co.uk

A CIP catalogue record for this book
is available from the British Library

ISBN 0 09 927459 0

Printed and bound in Great Britain by
Cox & Wyman Limited, Reading, Berkshire

To Clare Loveday

CONTENTS

ACKNOWLEDGEMENTS

Some of the stories in this collection have appeared in the following publications:

Scotland on Sunday; *Soho Square* (Bloomsbury); *Penguin 60* (Penguin); *Daily Telegraph*; *By the light of the Silvery Moon* (Virago); *W Magazine*; *Marie Claire*; *Woman and Home*; and *New Writing 6* (Vintage).

The Worlds Smallest Unicorn

'There's a parcel for you, Fan.'

'It'll be the toad lilies from the Spalding's catalogue,' she replied listlessly.

Teddy put the package addressed to his sister-in-law on the kitchen table, disappointed in his hope that some pleasure or good will might rub off it on to him and redeem his failure in the gift-bearing stakes. He hovered uneasily in the hostility emanating from Fan, aware of an antagonism caused by something more than his arrival the night before, with only two suitcases to show for his twenty years in Hong Kong. One contained his clothes, and the smaller held papers, a few books and socks and the sort of gewgaws you could find in any Chinese supermarket in London.

'Do stop hovering, Teddy. Sit down and I'll make some fresh toast. Tea or coffee? There's some green tea somewhere if you'd prefer. Or jasmine.'

'Coffee, please.'

Teddy sat on a chair too small for him, a fat man in a kingfisher-blue shantung suit. Fan's reaction to the parcel reminded him uncomfortably of a brown envelope and a clip round the ear long ago.

'Daddy! Dad! There's a letter for you.'

It was the raw noon of a motherless, shapeless Saturday.

3

Teddy tugged his father awake from tangled sheets, while his younger brother watched from the doorway, thumb in his mouth. Willie swore, snatching the letter. It turned out to be the final demand for the electricity bill and he ripped it in two, caught Teddy a stinging blow to the head and buried his face in his pillow again. In the light of experience, and Teddy wasn't feeling too good himself this morning, he could see that Willie had a hangover, but the stupid thing was he had known at the time that he was being disingenuous, a sly eleven-year-old who ought to have known better. He had hoped to earn his father's thanks by posing as a well-intentioned if mistaken lad, and he had got what he deserved. After Delia, the boys' mother, had left, the house was always cold, a snivelling cold that made them pull the sleeves of their jumpers over their hands and drag their cuffs across their noses, cold that chapped their lips and hurt their hair when they brushed it. Nothing was ever quite clean. The towels were damp and sticky and didn't dry you properly. Dirty clothes piled up in corners and homework was not done. Women came and went, and now and then the boys were treated to a slap-up meal at Bunjie's, that haunt of hobbits and folkies from time immemorial, but it wasn't the same.

Teddy and Webster Shelmerdine were the children of two musicians, Willie 'the Weeper' Shelmerdine and Delia MacFarlane. They grew up in the English jazz and folk revival of the Fifties and early Sixties, and although they had been named after Teddy Wilson and Ben Webster, they were weaned on skiffle and cut their teeth on Trad. Willie played the clarinet and sang, while Delia was primarily a singer who accompanied herself on washboard. She was also a semi-skilled harpist and harmonica player who could break your heart in the Gaelic at a ceilidh and twang out mouth-music when required. Willie and Delia were part of the scene, minor household names along with Pete and Peggy Seeger, Chas McDevitt and Nancy Whiskey, Chris Barber and Ottilie Patterson, partners in the tightly knit world of performers and fans on the jazz and folk circuit of gigs, festivals and clubs. Everybody knew all the gossip, and there was not a dry eye in the Green Man the night Willie bawled out 'Delia Gone' for the first time after she had run off with the jew's harp player from the Colin Clark City Stompers. Beryl Bryden, who was topping the bill, enfolded the weeping boys, Teddy and Webster, in the wings of her striped tent-dress like a hen comforting her chicks, but when they got home bleakness drifted like dust; 'Delia Gone' remained a crowd-pleaser, though.

> He comes down our alley and whistles me out.
> Before I get down there, he knocks me about.
> Still I love him, I'll forgive him,
> I'll go with him wherever he goes …

Delia used to sing, before Willie hit her one time too many and she rode that freight train, the 5.15 to Charing Cross, out of his life for ever.

'Don't bother with toast, Fan,' Teddy was saying, just as the bread jumped.

'You should have said if you didn't want it. I've made it now.'

'I do want it, thanks. I was just trying to save you the trouble.'

'It's hardly any trouble to bung two bits of bread in a toaster.' Her tone hinted at a hundred toastracks stretching as far back as the eye could see, all stacked with troubles caused by Teddy.

'I guess Web's gone to work. What about the girls?'

'Still in bed. Wasting the day.'

Fan wiped down the Dualit toaster and snapped at the cat as he came warily through his door, trying not to let it flap.

'And where do you think you've been, Mister? Sneaking in with your tail full of burrs, demanding breakfast at all hours.'

The cat, Rastus, attempted to catch Teddy's eye with a blokish wink, but he wasn't having any.

'Selfish little beasts, aren't they? Still, I suppose that's why we love them. The Cat that Walks by Himself and all that. Takes me back, I remember reading it to the kids years ago, last time I was home on leave. They've grown up into beautiful young ladies, Fan. A credit to you. A pair of real stunners, with the brains to match. You must be very proud of them.'

'I am.'

Fan ripped the lid from a tin of cat food, leaving Teddy feeling that he had said the wrong thing again. Of course, this time he was not home on leave, but redundant, an ex-employee of the Pink Panda Stationery Company billeted on Fan for the foreseeable, until he got back on his feet.

The summer holidays were almost over for Fan, a school secretary, and the girls, Bethan and Megan. Bethan was camping in Megan's room because bad Uncle Teddy had taken over hers. The spare room, where Teddy had slept nine years ago, was now a study filled with the family's computers and files and Webster's rowing machine. Teddy felt so tired as he replaced the lid on the Marmite and carried his plate and mug to the sink that he longed to crawl back into Bethan's bed, beneath the posters of vapid white boy bands and angry black gangstas, pull the duvet over his head, and sleep for a year. Perhaps for eternity.

'What are your plans for today?' Fan asked. 'You can leave those, I'll stick them in the dishwasher.'

Couldn't a man be allowed five minutes' jet lag after flying a quarter of the way round the globe? Did she have to make him feel completely useless by not even letting him wash up a few dishes?

'I – well, I thought I'd just – reorientate myself for a day or two – or re-occidentate myself, perhaps I should say. Put out a few feelers.'

'Like a beetle.'

Fan stared at Teddy in his suit, shot and nubbled with peacock threads.

'I suppose you had that suit made. In Honkers. I always wanted to do that, you know. Go shopping in Hong Kong and choose the material and have something made up just for me, to my own design. Something unique. Oh well, silly of me, I suppose. The paper's there if you want to have a look at it.'

'Thanks.'

Teddy picked up the newspaper obediently as Fan left the kitchen. What was he meant to do, turn straight to the Situations Vacant? How was he to have guessed that Fan had expected to be invited to stay? Perhaps that was what was eating her. Well, the stupid cow had had twenty years in which to suggest it. He wasn't a mind-reader. Just as well, though. Honkers! They would have wanted to eat in fancy restaurants and nightspots, demanded to see the 'real' Hong Kong and hoped to be taken to the Jockey Club or the FCC, where there was a waiting list for membership and where Teddy had dined only once as a guest in all the years he had lived there. He certainly wouldn't have wanted to introduce them to his own watering hole, the Hong Kong Skittles Club, a sporting establishment mostly in name, with its sour clientèle of disappointed ex-pats. The Skittles' dullness suited him; he had become accustomed to it, and protective of it, and he shuddered at the thought of Web and Fan fumbling with their chopsticks in its little dining room, before contracting food poisoning, or sitting at the bar in shorts and sandals, Fan sipping some touristy cocktail with a parasol and Web droning on about small-bore cooling systems for automatic hand-dryers and hustling for orders for his light-engineering firm. Even so, Teddy could kick himself for not having brought Fan a dress or a jacket, or even a length of silk. A bad move to present her with that plastic fan last night, whipping it open with a flourish, 'A fan for Fan, from your greatest fan.' He winced at the memory, and that obsolete Pink Panda stock, the rulers and rubbers and little notebooks and cute panda stickers, had proved quite unsuitable for two young ladies who had done so spectacularly well in their exams, although they'd liked the miniature cameras with scenes of Hong Kong by night and the fortune cookies, waterflowers and joss sticks, unless they were just being kind or sending him up.

'How sad to think of people spending their lives making these things,' Fan had remarked.

Even if he had brought Fan something to wear, he'd have

got the size wrong, knowing his luck, because he couldn't help noticing she'd put on the beef a bit. Fan was fair and slimmish now rather than skinny, and still favoured the droopy English look of faded Aertex blouse, or polo shirt, cotton skirt and cardy. Teddy could never quite decide whether it was sexy or not. It was a world away from the gloss and gilt and sharp edges of the women he was used to. He turned the pages of the *Independent* abstractedly. Maybe he could pick something up for Fan in Chinatown and pretend he'd had it in his suitcase, although he'd have to be careful; his pitiful pay-off from the Pink Panda Stationery Company wouldn't stretch far. Teddy's only lasting contribution to the firm which had 'rationalized' him in preparation for the Chinese take-over was to be found in its name.

'With respect, Mr Tang, a company that designates itself "stationary" is a company that is going nowhere,' he had told the firm's founder at his interview. 'No wonder Pink Panda's profits are at a standstill.' Well, he could see it was a tinpot outfit, but gradually they had turned it round and moved the factory into better premises. The trouble was, as young Tangs, sons, daughters, and cousins, grew up and the extended family was brought into the business, Teddy was passed over for promotion time and time again. It was only Mr Tang's residual loyalty that kept him in the office at all, and by the time he left he was an anachronism known simply as 'the *Gweilo*', a word meaning ghost as well as foreigner; a bad spirit to be exorcised.

Fan's head poked round the door, saying, 'If you've got any washing, dump it in the dirty-linen basket in the bathroom. I'll be doing a mixed load later.'

Notes from a flute spiralled down the stairs.

'Who's playing? Not the kids, surely?' said Teddy.

'Oh, the twins have been tootling on their flutes since they were two jampots high.' Fan was dismissive, as though he ought, as an uncle, to have known that.

'Ah well, blood will out,' said Teddy.

Delia's grandfather had been a Nigerian-Scots seaman from Port Glasgow, and her granddaughters Bethan and Megan had taken her pale delicate features and replicated her dark eyes and charcoal cloud of hair in blue and gold. They wore their own hair in cascades of long thin braids, but, as Fan's father had put it at their christening, you would never guess that those two little English rosebuds had a touch of the tarbrush. Unless you had a more educated eye than his. Webster was green-eyed and freckled, while Teddy was white, with disconcertingly opaque eyes like black olives under heavy lids, and their hair, the russet and the black, kinked into wool from unravelled jumpers if it was not kept short.

Teddy was thinking about his nieces. Sixteen years old. It didn't seem possible. So many birthdays he had missed. He couldn't get over how they'd changed, the sheer length of the pale golden legs and thighs in tiny black shorts and the briefest swirl of skirt, the smooth distances of flesh between croptop and navel and waistband, the long, long slender arms flailing from tight-ribbed short sleeves. Even for twins, between them they seemed to have more than their allocation of limbs, and was there really any need for them to be so tall, he wondered. After all, it was not as though they had to reach up to pull the topmost leaves from a drought-stricken tree in order to survive, was it? 'How tall they've grown,' he had said on meeting them last night, and reminded them how he had once read *The Jumblies* to them, one perched on each knee in their pyjamas.

> And in twenty years they all came back,
>   In twenty years or more,
> And every one said, 'How tall they've grown! ...

Except that it was he who had come back after twenty years, minus a couple of short breaks, he who was the Jumbly, or some poor toeless Pobble or wandering luminous-nosed Dong, shuffling home like a disgraced Behemoth. And everyone thought, how fat he's grown. There was an Edward Lear print, of a salmon-crested cockatoo, in the dining room. He had remarked on it during one of the silences which had fallen between the clash of eating implements and the twins' fits of the giggles.

'What's it like in Hong Kong, Uncle Teddy?'

'Well, depends where you mean. There's Hong Kong side and Kowloon side and –'

'Can you speak Chinese, Uncle Teddy? Cantonese and Mandarin?'

'And Satsuma and Clementine? And Grapefruit?'

'That's enough,' said Fan. 'Be your age.'

Teddy said, 'In Wan Chai, where I live, lived –'

'That's the old Suzy Wong district, isn't it?' put in Webster, with what Fan perceived as a leer.

'That's right. You've got lots of narrow streets and bars and clubs. There's the Pussy Cat and the Hotlips, they're mainly pick-up joints, topless, I believe, and the Wanch, which is a mock pub run by *gweilos*, foreigners, for *gweilos*.'

The girls were stuffing napkins into their mouths.

Fan said, 'There must be more to it than that. A more salubrious side. It can't all be sleaze.'

She heard the tinkle of temple bells above the traffic's roar in a street teeming with limousines, rickshaws, buffalo-carts and bicycles ridden by people in conical hats under skyscrapers festooned with ideographed banners.

'Oh, of course. There are the artisans' streets where you can buy anything in the world you might want. The street of the coffin-makers for example, the street of the metal-beaters, the street of the tailors, all sorts. And people sitting on chairs on the pavement who do every kind of repair, shoes, rattan furniture, clothes; and old grandmothers selling matches, watchstraps …'

'Fake Rolexes,' said the twins.

Teddy glanced at his watch, acknowledging his dereliction of avuncular duty.

'The architecture's fascinating, Fan, you'd love it. And it's a very safe city to walk about in.'

'Oh, good.'

'What about the Triads?' Megan asked.

'We've got Triads at our school,' said Bethan.

'Don't be so ridiculous!' Fan lost patience. 'As if Miss O'Nions would tolerate such a thing! I don't know why you're showing off like a couple of three-year-olds.'

The twins rolled their eyes heavenwards with pitying sighs.

'So have you got many Chinese friends now or did you mostly hang out with the ex-pats?' said Webster.

'Well, a few. The Chinese don't really like us much. And most of the ex-pats are a pretty dull bunch. The sort of people who knew they would never make it here and imagined they'd be big fish in a small pool, and then became embittered and turned to hard drinking when they weren't.'

Teddy realized that they might think he was describing himself. Fan thought of fish bumping each other in crowded tanks in Chinese takeaways. She burst out harshly, 'But they're a cruel people, aren't they, the Chinese? Cruel to each other, and to animals. I mean, look at all those endangered species they grind up for their herbal medicines.'

'They're very fond of birds,' Teddy told her. 'Devoted to them. Everywhere you go, in the streets, on buses and the MTR and the ferries, you see people with their pet birds. Little ·finches mostly.'

'You mean they carry them on their shoulders, or walk them on leads? I suppose they have to, if they've eaten all the dogs.'

'In cages,' said Teddy.

'Mum rests her case,' said Megan.

Bethan said, 'Mum, I never knew you were such a racist.'

Now, in the bedroom, Fan stared out of the window and remembered the unpleasant evening. The girls had been at their silliest, embarrassingly middle class. Not that she thought they *should* be working in a sweatshop or topless bar like girls half their age in Hong Kong, but you never knew where you were with them these days; one minute they were clamouring to be allowed to stay at clubs until six o'clock in the morning, the next behaving like spoiled brats. She didn't know what Teddy would think, not that she cared about impressing him. She saw that the Michaelmas daisies, those harbingers of autumn, were in flower and it occurred to her that they always seemed to be out nowadays. Everywhere you looked, people were going on about the melting of the polar ice-cap, and hurtling towards the Millennium, but maybe the Michaelmas daisies only indicated the swift passing of her own years. Whatever, it appeared likely that she would spend her personal *fin de siècle*, picking up other folks' dirty clothes. No sooner had she shaken the sand of Cyprus from the holiday suitcases, than along came Teddy, the bad penny, the hole in the head, to dump another peck of dirt on her. She had returned from their self-catering villa looking forward to pottering about in a leisurely way before the start of term, and now here was this succubus squatting in her kitchen, expecting to be fed. She wondered if he had found yet the item in the paper which she hoped he would encounter with a shock. A double-take of disbelief. A stab of grief. A pang of guilt.

She watched Rastus shredding the trunk of the lilac tree with his claws. The garden was full of seed-heads, thistledown, parachutes, exploded pods and burnt-out rockets. The green bunches of ash keys were tinged with red and mildewed damsons lay scattered on the grass. It would soon be time to put the bulbs in. 'Forever Autumn', she thought, but another song was playing insistently through her head, one she had always hated, about Willie the Weeper who made his living as a chimney sweeper. Well, if Willie Shelmerdine had ever swept his own chimney, that terraced house in Blackheath, so convenient for the Green Man, might be standing now. As might Willie. What a dead loss as a grandfather he had been. And as for that reprobate runaway grandma, Delia Gone, the old trout, now finally departed and good riddance, she had become a romantic figure to the twins, who insisted on claiming their one-sixteenth part of African heritage, apeing the hairstyles and speech of their black classmates and spelling Africa with a k.

Fan sat on the bed, averting her glance from her reflection in the wardrobe door. Trust Teddy to pitch up when sun, salt and sand had frayed her hair to rope, and haloumi and feta and Cypriot wine had taken their toll. The irony was, she had been feeling relaxed and attractive, languorous and at ease with Webster in their late-summer lovemaking, until Teddy had arrived to diminish her. And yet he was no oil painting himself, no spring chicken either. She had been practically at screaming point last night, waiting for a moment alone with him, and had gone bitterly to bed at last, leaving him and Webster chortling over old times with the bottle of duty-free Jack Daniels, and Teddy stubbing out cigarettes in the saucer Webster had provided, one of the few left from their wedding tea service.

And this morning, when they were at last alone, he had just sat there eating toast in that bright blue suit. Enraged as she was by Teddy, Fan despised herself more, because she had to admit that if Teddy had shown by a word or a look or a covert touch of his hand that he desired her still, she would have forgiven him. He was pathetic. All the fat fool had to do was to tell her she hadn't changed a bit, or that she was more beautiful than ever, and he was too dumb to realize it. Of course she was proud of the girls, but to have Teddy Shelmerdine, an adulterer who had slept with his own brother's wife, treat her like some mumsy hausfrau was more than she could bear.

It was a sultry day, nine years ago, the grey sky full of static electricity and little grumbles of thunder. The children had been taken to the cinema by the mother of one of their friends. With the passing of time, Fan had managed to put that afternoon out of her mind, but every now and then her conscience, responding to some stimulus, flashed an ugly scene into her mind. In a red desert landscape, two beasts, coarse-haired, four-footed, ungulant, were pawing the dust, raising their snouts to sniff the scent of distant rain, circling and circling a tree, whose uneasy leaves shivered in the dry wind that ruffled a ridge of bristles along their spines. They got closer and closer, tusk to flank, until with a grunt they were coupling blindly in a stinging red sandstorm of tumbleweed and broken cactus spikes, and raindrops as flat and heavy as stones.

But it hadn't really been like that at all, ochreous, ruttish, with nostrils dilating in the sulphurous air, splayed hooves, and curved tusks gripping her back, the afternoon that two palish mammals had sheltered from the storm in the spare-room bed. Teddy had been tender and sweet; Fan had cried,

and for a while imagined that she had married the wrong
brother.

The following day Teddy had been driven to the airport by
the doubly betrayed and unsuspecting Webster, with the
kids in the back singing along to an old ABBA tape. Fan
waited in vain for a phone call, she searched for a coded
message in the postcard that arrived at last, thanking them
for having him to stay, she half-dreaded but yearned for a
mysterious bouquet from Interflora, with no card. Then she
fell into a dark and unexplainable depression. Teddy had
forced her to reappraise herself and to discover that she was
not the high-principled person she had thought herself to be,
caring and competent and so clever in presenting her
husband with a pair of bright-as-a-button twins. She had
slept with two people in her life, both of them Shelmerdines.
What a track record. Why not make it a hat trick with old
Willie? A grey year passed before she seemed to be her old
self again. Teddy Shelmerdine had stolen a year from her,
and from her family, while she wore those fog-tinted
spectacles of despair, and he was not gentleman enough to
pretend that he was still carrying a torch, or that the episode
had meant anything to him at all.

The girls had switched on the radio in their room, with
the sound considerably low.

'For God's sake turn up that bloody noise!' Fan shouted.

'I can hear myself think!'

'Sorry, Mum.'

And the volume was turned down.

Fan kicked one of Webster's unassuming shoes under the bed, furious with him for being so pleased to see his big brother, as if he had been the failure of the family and Teddy the success. Webster had looked so hurt and disappointed in her last night when, needled beyond endurance, she had taken advantage of Teddy's trip to the bathroom to remark, 'Typical of Teddy to turn tail and run as soon as things get a bit rough out there.'

'When the going gets tough, the tough get going. Isn't that what your Mrs Thatcher used to say?' Teddy came back into the room.

'She was never "our" Mrs Thatcher. If it comes to that, she was yours as much as ours.'

'Fan! Have you seen this, in the paper?'

Teddy ran up the stairs, holding on to the banister on the landing to get his breath.

'Did you see this about Lola Henriques?'

'The singer? Wasn't she an old flame of yours? What about her?'

Teddy saw Lola's face in the flare of a cigarette lighter. Yes, she was an old flame of his.

'She's dead. The funeral's today, at Golders Green. Has

20

Web got a black tie I can borrow?'

The girls had come out on to the landing, wearing the big T-shirts they slept in, which scarcely covered their minuscule pants.

'For goodness sake put some clothes on,' said Fan, 'lolling around half-naked at this time of day.'

To Teddy, she said, 'I saw her on the telly a few months ago, in some documentary, can't remember what it was about, but I do recall remarking to Webster at the time that she didn't look well.'

'Lola never looked well. It was part of her charm.'

'There's a black tie somewhere, I think.'

Fan went into the marital bedroom and came back dangling a black knotted noose.

'Here you are. Actually, I believe it was your father's.'

'Uncle Teddy,' said Megan, 'we're like really sorry about – you know, the funeral – and that.'

'Thank you, Megan.'

Fan followed Teddy into his room.

'Do you think this shirt's all right? Not too tight?' he asked.

'Let me look. Hmmm. Have you tried the pencil test?'

'The pencil test?'

'Oh, it's just something people used to do, to see if they could go without a bra. You put a pencil under your breast, and if it falls out, you're OK.'

21

Teddy looked at her with his black olive eyes whose expression she could never read.

'I'd better get going. Don't bother about lunch, I'll pick something up on the way.'

'This isn't Hong Kong, you know, with noodle-sellers on every street corner and people ringing little bells to advertise their wares.'

After he had gone, Fan booked herself a hair appointment and decided to go into school the following day to prepare for the new term. The thought of the bewildered new intake in their big blazers calmed her down.

Teddy was sitting on the red bench at the bus stop outside Chik'N'Ribs, waiting for a bus to Brixton tube station, and watching three pigeons playing spillikins with somebody's lunch on the pavement, taking turns to stab a chip with their beaks and send it flying into the gutter. Spillikins, Jack Straws, Pik-a-stik, whatever you called the game, the ratio of potato to effort was minimal. Teddy saw that one of the players was handicapped by the loss of a foot, and he wondered if the number of discarded takeaways at such a short distance from Chik'N'Ribs was an indictment of its cuisine, or whether most of its clientèle were simply too drunk to finish their meals. To his left sat a man of about his own age with the rough red skin and tormented, boiled-sweet stare of the heavy drinker, and to his right, as far away as possible, a young black woman glanced up from time to time from the gospel text she was reading to see if a bus was coming. The greasy smell of warm meat drove any thought of his own lunch from Teddy's mind.

It was hot now, and traffic and people pushing buggies hung about with children toiled up and down the hill in fumy sunshine splintered by the drills of roadworks and thumped by music from passing cars. The engine of a parked lorry throbbed like a thousand headaches and the sirens of a posse of police cars swooped and looped the loop; the leaden air had an aggressive edge. This had never been a wealthy area, but Teddy could not help noticing the general atmosphere of defeat, how much poorer and shabbier the people looked since he was last there, how many shops were boarded up. Evidently the news that the recession was over had not reached these parts yet.

A bus marked 'Sorry Not In Service' raised false hopes for a moment. Teddy lit a cigarette. A small crowd had formed at the bus stop. Apparently queueing was a thing of the past. He had been waiting fifteen minutes now and he remembered how often he had set out on some journey in good spirits, only to have his heart broken by the transport system of south London. They ordered these things much better in Hong Kong. Teddy suddenly felt homesick, an exile in his own land. He dared not think about the future. He did not want to think about Lola; time enough for that at the crematorium. He thought about Fan. How bad-tempered she had become. Perhaps she was getting menopausal, that might explain it. They'd hit it off so well last time he was home. Her attitude of sarcasm and contempt couldn't, surely it couldn't, have anything to do with that afternoon when they'd been alone in the house? So far as he recalled, it had been great. A bit of fun. She'd had no complaints then. Surely she didn't expect — surely she was as anxious to forget the whole thing as he was? After all, they'd both been a lot younger then. So much water had flowed under the bridge for all of them, and his life was complicated enough already without dragging up the past.

If a train came right away at Brixton, and if he didn't have to wait long for a Golders Green train at Euston, he might still just make it. Two useless buses came and went. Ought he to get some flowers? Why were there no taxis? No wonder everybody looked so ground down. Twenty-five minutes now. Didn't anybody give a damn that there might be someone in a hurry to see an old flame consigned to — to pay his last respects? It was when a funeral cortège going up the hill to Norwood Cemetery stopped at the lights, displaying a floral tribute which spelled out NAN in pink and white letters, that Teddy gave up hope and turned away from the bus stop. What did he know of Lola's life anyway, and there would be people there he didn't want to meet, who would think him fat and seedy and wonder what Lola had ever seen in him, and remember that he had treated her shabbily. Just as well he hadn't bought any flowers, but then again, he supposed he could have given them to Fan. Teddy went into a florist's shop, and on his way out, his eye was caught by a brightly coloured poster for Zippos Circus on the boarded-up shop next door. Across the bottom of the poster was written, SEE THE WORLDS SMALLEST UNICORN & THE FANTASTIC CONTORTION OF MADAME ZSA-ZSA!

Teddy felt he could live without Madame Zsa-Zsa's contortion, but the world's smallest unicorn, that would be something to behold. How big would it be? He pictured a miniature beast, milk-white, with a horn fluted like a conical seashell, nestling in the palm of the ringmaster's hand. Or perhaps it would be larger, trotting round the ring, wearing the golden medieval collar of a unicorn kneeling beside a maiden in a tapestry. Then he thought, you fool. The unicorn is a mythical beast. There is no such animal as the unicorn, big or small. It is heraldic, it battles with lions in nursery rhymes, it is rampant on shields and attracted to virgins. Disappointed, and feeling foolish, he turned away. Zippo's unicorn would turn out to be a Shetland pony with something glued to its head, or a bonsai-ed goat whose horns had gone wrong, and fused into one protuberance. Just as well he had realized his mistake before buying a family ticket and trundling them all off to Streatham Common. A convoy of buses passed him, the 196, two 2s and a 322, all going to Brixton. He sat for a while in Norwood Cemetery, out of sight of the funeral, and asked Lola to forgive him for not making it to hers, the flowers he had bought to placate Fan beside him on the bench. The Chinese sent their dead off into the afterlife equipped with everything they might need, cars, computers, fridges, stereos, microwaves, you name it, all made of paper, and he hadn't even managed a flower for Lola. Sitting there, psyching himself up to return to the house, he felt as much of a *gweilo* as he ever had in Hong Kong, as lonely as a ghost. He dreaded the thought of a succession of nights in Bethan's room with her posters and make-up and cuddly toys. The Chinese were probably right, the smaller and more crowded the room, the less space there was for ghosts.

Teddy let himself in with the spare key Webster had given him, and went straight upstairs. There, in the doorway of Bethan's room, with a bunch of funereal white gladioli in his hand, he confronted an extraordinary tableau. Megan stood with a sandwich halfway to her mouth, Bethan was kneeling, stilled in the act of scrabbling through an untidy drawer, and beside his open suitcase was Fan with a tiny black silk slip in one hand and a framed photograph in the other.

'What's this?' she said.

'No idea — mix-up at the laundry I suppose. Never seen it before in my life.'

26

'No, this! Who's this in the photograph?'

The girls crowded her to look. The picture was of a boy, a smiling boy about ten years old with almond-shaped eyes. A beautiful boy.

'His name's William,' Teddy said.

'He's your son, isn't he?'

Fan sat down on the bed, still holding the photograph.

'You bastard,' she said. 'I was looking for your dirty washing and I found it.'

Bethan took the picture from her.

'You mean, he's like – our cousin?'

'He is your cousin,' Teddy said.

Fan burst into tears, weeping like a monarch who has been brought the news of the loss of a colony, but the twins were staring at Teddy over the photograph frame as if at a shining island rising out of the sea on the horizon.

Crossing the Border

Flora had never been so far south. She was driving past sari shops, silk wholesalers, sweetshops and sweatshops, restaurants and jewellers, through a low-rise landscape broken by spires and temples and mosques, in Sunday afternoon traffic puffing out bouquets of January gloom. Her own second-hand Metro was fuelled by a mixture of anticipation and doubt. Long streets of stuccoed terraced houses curved away on either side of the road, and then the red-brick pagoda of a Tesco superstore reared up and blue galvanized warehouses and DIY emporia, and now she was in the half-timbered hinterland, where London ebbs into the pampas grass and mock-Tudor of the edge of Kent, taking the wrong turning at a roundabout.

When Flora had left home, the dark bobbles of the plane trees in the square where she lived were draggling like trimmings of frowsty curtains in a sky of mushroom soup. Now, as the road petered out into a rutted track and she stopped the car, the sun licked through the glutinous grey, revealing streaks of pale-blue glaze and linking a gold necklace of dazzling puddles. Across a small field, behind the bare twigs of oak trees, Flora could see what must be the backs of the houses in the road she had missed, Bourne Avenue. At the field's edge, an angler was fishing in a pond encircled with barbed wire where white geese swam, and two booted and anoraked women walked past with seven or eight dogs leaping between them. Flora stepped out into a mild composty wind and locked the car. Elders and wooden fence posts were emerald with winter damp. She picked her way over gravel and mud, telling herself that ten minutes more would make no difference to Great-Uncle Lorimer after all these years. To her left, in a thin tangled wood, here and there the massive trunk of a felled oak sported a crown of new pale antlers. Flora tripped on a root and reflected that she was, in a sense, seeking her own roots, tracing a branch of her family tree. There was a tape recorder in the bag on her shoulder.

Her chief interest lay in her late Great-Uncle Laurence, the poet, and she was hoping that his brother Lorimer would give her insights into and anecdotes from the shared childhood of the two sons of the manse who had taken such different paths. She, like her great-uncles, was among those of the large Looney family who had dropped the second 'o' from their name. Uncle Lorimer had reverted to the original for reasons of his own. Flora, whose father was a poet of a different kind from Laurence, a corduroy-jacketed, much-married journeyman, had determined to write the biography of Laurence Loney, who had died alone in a trailer park in Nevada, and she had got as far as her title, *Tumbleweed and Whin*. It encapsulated, she felt, the unhappy, contradictory character of the author of *Poor Pink Trash* and *Behind the Scones at the Tattoo*. Like Laurence, she was moved by ephemera and junk and saw eternity in a plastic flower and the human condition in the brittle pink Little Princess Vanity Set in the supermarket, whose tiny mirror flashed a fragment of dream. The bleached bones of a bird or a skull in the heather spoke to her too, as plaintively as a peewit or the pale torso of a lost Barbie doll.

The tips of birches made a rosy haze in the distance against a sky growing colder and Flora could hear the chilly sound of running water. Squelching into the wood, she discovered a swift stream carrying leaves and little gnarled alder fruits between its steep banks. A middle-aged man with a red setter was approaching and, surmising that he was not a murderer, Flora called out, 'Is there a bridge across this stream?'

'Stream? This is the Ravensbourne river!'

A stalwart local historian, Flora recognized, as the dog scrambled into the water, splashing against the current in a whirligig of red feathery ears and tail and radiant droplets, and the man followed it upstream. Flora returned to the path and walked on, encountering several more of these unfriendly, not-quite-country folk, until she found herself on the verge of a pick-your-own smallholding, where strawberry plants huddled in rain-spangled furrows of black plastic, by a makeshift shelter of corrugated tin and polythene where the strawberries were weighed in the summer. Time to turn back, but there was something shimmering and dazzling at the end of the track, with bright flashes of moving colours.

It was a heap, a low mountain, of shining straw mucked out from stables, glinting gilt and copper and brass in the sun as Flora drew near, its stalks clogged with horse manure, and on its peak stood a cockerel, red-gold and viridescent. Guinea fowl, turkeys, cocks and hens and ornamental pheasants pecked about on the pungent slopes and ridges of the magic midden, astonishing and entrancing Flora with their display of drooping shot-silk tail feathers, yellow chinoiserie, scarlet and coral combs and cloisonné plumage.

While she had been wandering in that strange landscape, Flora had been able to forget herself, and to flinch only slightly when her rebuffed smiles fell like dying butterflies into the mud, but the mirror in the car brought her abruptly back to Flora Loney, aged twenty-seven, wind-smudged and damp, lips chafed, blue eyes watering, fair hair in clumps of straw on the shoulders of her coat, black ankle boots stained and black tights speckled and a smear of dirt across one unusually pink cheekbone. Yes, she looked inescapably like Flora, blurred, anxious, untidy and late, with new footwear ruined by a careless impulse. If Great-Uncle Lorimer had not been expecting her, she would have gone straight home, carrying with her the picture of those exotic birds on the golden dunghill as sufficient adventure for one day. She reversed along the track, splashing a sullen couple in woolly hats, negotiated the turning into Bourne Avenue and found a parking space. She walked up the path on her long black legs under her short black coat as nervously as a little girl going to a party, with her tape recorder in her bag, clutching a paper cone of orange spray carnations.

The house looked ordinary enough, Edwardian, double-fronted, with dull green paint and windows looking out on to wintry shrubs and the tips of bulbs, but what had she expected, a bunch of balloons bobbing on the gate, a bucket of whitewash balanced on the porch? She took a deep breath and pushed the bell, heard its tired voice in the interior, and waited, contemplating an umbrella like an injured fruitbat. Footsteps shuffled and the door was opened by an old woman in purple pompommed slippers, with her hair piled in an elaborate confection of peroxide peaks and swirls on top of her head, circles of rouge on white powdered cheeks and a crimson mouth in which her own lips were lost somewhere. Giggling with relief, Flora said, 'I can see I've come to the right house!'

'What do you mean?'

'Grimaldi House. The Home for Retired Clowns.'

'Next door,' said the woman, shutting her own in Flora's face, which burst into flames of embarrassment and guilt.

Flora could have wept at her own ill-judged verbal custard pie. 'Me and my big mouth,' she thought, fishing in her pocket for a stub of lipsalve and applying it to her frayed lips. She could no more make amends than she could have eaten her words at the dinner party the night before, when she had remarked, 'A fettucine worse than death,' as her hostess put down the dish. After that everything, including the soufflé that followed, had fallen rather flat. Flora was almost at the gate when she heard, 'Miss!'

She turned, ready to attempt an apology.

'I doubt if they'll take you. Why don't you try a different career instead? Apply for one of those government retraining schemes?'

'Yes, thanks. I might do that. Good idea,' Flora was bleating as the door snapped shut again.

The name on the gate was Grimsby Lodge. Grimaldi House was indeed the house next door. But the false clowness had been nearer the mark than she knew. A few years earlier Flora had been one of only two students, in a class of thirty-five studying circus skills, who had failed to graduate. Just one more smallish shame in a lifetime of fumbled catches and dropped opportunities. How right Daddy had been to suggest that Flora was a little unbalanced even to contemplate the high wire, and how smug he had been when she had fallen off. Since she had flunked circus skills, she had seen former classmates coining it in from the crowds in Covent Garden, and once, broke, desperate and behind with the rent, Flora had set up with her juggling balls on someone else's pitch, only to be pelted from the Piazza. Her fellow-failure, a young woman named Ziggy Deville, with whom Flora was superficially friendly, now had her own column on a newspaper which paid her vast sums of money to write about her hangovers, discarded diets, disastrous love life and the drug-related deaths of her flatmates.

A sad-faced visitor was leaving Grimaldi House as Flora arrived and he held the front door open for her, admitting her to the hall, where she tinkled the ceramic handbell that stood under a vase of beige silk roses next to the visitors' book. Flora glanced at the page, hoping to recognize some illustrious showbiz name, and saw that somebody had drawn a smiley face by way of signature. She waited apprehensively, inhaling a potpourri of late-afternoon ennui, tea in plastic beakers and air-freshener. A portrait of the great Grimaldi hung on the wall, opposite a garish and rather tactless print of a clown with a downturned mouth and a teardrop oozing from his painted eye. Televisions rumbled behind doors, cutlery clashed in a distant steel sink. Eventually a small woman of Far-Eastern mien, in a pink overall, appeared.

'Can I help you?'

'Oh, yes, thank you. I've come to see my Great-Uncle Lorimer. He's expecting me. I wrote.'

The woman stared at Flora.

'Looney the Clown,' Flora added helpfully.

'Oh dear. If you'd like to just take a seat in the visitors' lounge.'

A white door was closed behind Flora. She sat on the chintz sofa wondering what the pink-overalled woman had meant: *if* Flora just took a seat, would Great-Uncle Lorimer be wheeled in to her in a chair like the one she had seen folded in the hall; would she be led into a roomful of clowns in full motley and be expected to pick out the right one? She hadn't seen Looney since she was three and had been carried screaming back to her seat after she had rushed into the circus ring to batter with her tiny fists the clown who tipped a bucket of yellow paint down Looney's trousers. Would she just be left sitting here until she was old enough to be wheeled away herself? Not daring to try the door in case it was locked, Flora combated her panic by deep breathing. Nobody knew she was here. She had told nobody of her mission that afternoon. She tried to concentrate on the hand-stitched Serenity Prayer on the wall, but found herself thinking about a friend who had lost a toe in the throes of a charismatic church service in the Brompton Road, and she turned to study a signed poster of the Cottle Sisters' Circus. Grimaldi House was, she knew, a benevolent institution founded by a famous circus family and maintained by voluntary contributions and fund-raising activities. Flora recalled seeing a minibus without wheels in the front garden. The residents of Grimaldi House weren't going anywhere, it seemed. She began to worry about the woman in the pink overall, and wondered if she were a prisoner too. A Filipina child-prostitute, tricked into a fake marriage, and held as a suburban slave, possibly even a sex-slave, in a house of dotard clowns.

Was it her duty to help the woman to escape? Ziggy Deville would know what to do, if she were here and she could then expose the whole racket in her newspaper column. If only she had a mobile, she could call Ziggy now. Except that she'd probably be asleep or too hungover to speak or in bed with somebody, or dead or something. Flora heard the desolate buzzing and thumping of a vacuum cleaner, such a bleak sound on a Sunday afternoon, and an old man droning out, 'If you don't want the whelks, don't muck 'em abaht,' over and over again, until Flora felt lost on a timeless foreshore made up of whelk shells ceaselessly shifting with the tide. She was about to try the door when it opened and a tall, fair woman in a brown and beige jacquard dress came in.

'I'm Mrs Endersby. Sit down again, won't you, my dear? That's right. I'm afraid I've got some rather sad news for you. Your poor dear uncle slipped away from us in the early hours of this morning.'

'How?' said Flora, dazedly picturing a clown sliding like a shadow under a sash window into the pre-dawn darkness and shinning down a drainpipe. 'He was expecting me. I wrote. I really need to talk to him. I'm his brother's official biographer. Sort of.'

'I'm afraid he just couldn't hang on any longer, dear. He was already very frail, and an infection in somebody of his age — well ... Of course the sixty cigarettes a day for all those years, until he came to us, had taken their toll ...'

Flora gazed at Mrs Endersby. It was the first time she had actually seen somebody wearing that dress advertised on the back pages of tabloid Sunday supplements, with smart gilt-effect buttons and matching belt-buckle trim. She realized that she was sitting on her flowers.

'Am I being thick?' she asked. 'I mean, are you trying to tell me that Great-Uncle Lorimer is dead?'

'I'm so sorry, my dear. I would have hoped that you might have been saved a journey – some of the other relatives have collected his bits and pieces, and the gentlemen from Messrs Chappell are in charge of the Arrangements. They gave one of our long-term "Grimaldis" a lovely circus send-off recently, with a dear little baby elephant pulling the hearse. Perhaps you saw it on *Newsroom South-East*? Oh, no, you wouldn't have, you've come all the way down from Scotland, haven't you? Such a shame.'

'Indirectly', said Flora. There was no way she was going to ask which of the relatives had collected Lorimer's 'bits and pieces'. There were so many, and any one of them was capable of pipping her at the post in the biography stakes, given half a chance. Poor old Looney. She knew his funeral would not make the local news and that Mrs Endersby knew it too and despised them all accordingly. She hadn't even let him smoke, poor old bugger, probably not even an exploding cigar for old times' sake.

'He wouldn't want you to upset yourself,' said Mrs Endersby. 'Dear old Looney, we'll miss him. He was always such a merry soul, never complained. Are you in the profession yourself? No, I thought not. Never mind, I'm sure our

Looney's got them all in fits up in heaven now!'

'I bet you say that to all the girls,' Flora muttered as Mrs Endersby cocked an ear ceilingwards as if to catch the gales of angelic laughter. All Flora could hear was, 'If you don't want the whelks, don't muck 'em abaht.'

'Doesn't that man ever sing anything else?' she asked, taking a tissue from a conveniently sited box.

'Oh, that's our Corky. Quite a card is our Corky. Keeps us on our toes, bless him,' she added grimly. 'Oh, I almost forgot. Looney left something for you. He was most particular you should have it. I'll just ask Mrs Ho to fetch it before you go.'

She left the door open as she went into the hall and shook the little bell. Flora heard an exasperated female voice say, 'Put it away now, Chippy. It's not clever and it's not funny.'

Flora's heart was beating faster. Great-Uncle Lorimer had thought of her at the last. If only she hadn't put off the visit.

Mrs Endersby returned, followed by the sex-slave, now identified as Mrs Ho, carrying a white cardboard box. Flora took it awkwardly.

'Aren't you going to open it?' asked Mrs Endersby.

'See what your uncle give you,' Mrs Ho encouraged.

Flora hesitated. Mrs Ho was probably very keen on ancestors and would think that Flora was dishonouring Great-Uncle Lorimer by her lack of enthusiasm, but she was afraid to open the box. It was as if she might find Uncle Lorimer inside, shrunk to the size of a doll or a mummified monkey in a

41

clown's costume. She prised up a corner, then lifted the lid. On a bed of faded pink tissue paper lay a pair of clown's shoes.

Cradling the box like a baby she hadn't wanted, Flora said, 'I wonder why ...'

A younger woman, in pale blue, hurried in, saying, 'Sorry to butt in, but could you come please, Mrs Endersby? There's been an incident in the Big Top!'

Flora followed them into the hall and saw, through a half-open door at the end of the corridor, old men in dressing gowns slumped on a circle of chairs under the bright circus mural running round the walls.

Mrs Endersby, excusing herself, strode towards the Big Top. Mrs Ho showed Flora out.

As she sat in the car, hoping that her orange carnations, which she had left on the sofa in the visitors' lounge, would perk up in water and give pleasure to the poor souls in the Big Top, but suspecting that they would find a home in Mrs Endersby's sanctum, a minicab drew up beside her. As it reversed, Flora glimpsed a white masklike face at the passenger window. She pulled away quickly. So it had been Great-Uncle Lorimer's room that they were Hoovering. She remembered a children's television programme showing how clowns register their make-up by painting it on eggs which are then stored in the vault of a special clowns' church in the East End of London. What was the copyright on a greasepaint smile, Flora wondered, ten years, fifty years, a hundred years, eternity? Or, in an East End crypt tonight, would an eggshell be ceremoniously smashed?

'Oh no, not clown shoes! I must be in for some pretty bad news!' Flora's mother, Ella said, when Flora telephoned her that evening.

'What do you mean, Mother? I've just *given* you some pretty bad news.'

'It's a song, "Clown Shoes". I've been trying to remember the words for years, and who it was by. Was it Johnny Burnett? Anyway, darling, of course it's sad about Lorimer, but he had a good innings, or whatever clowns have, and I hardly knew him. He *was* your *father*'s uncle, you know. Anyway, in the song, this girl sends her boyfriend a pair of clown shoes to tell him they're through. It's hilarious — as if sending clown shoes was standard protocol. Do you think there was a special clowns' shoe department in the shoe store, or that they had to buy them from a circus? Anyway, it ends up with the boy putting the clown shoes on. Sad. Can't you just see the High School Hop, with all the Jilted Johns bopping around in clown shoes?'

'No, Mother. I'd better ring Daddy.'

'Poor Looney. I wonder what they did with his wig. It was green. Looney was a punk before his time. I wonder if that's where Keith got it from.'

'Of course he didn't.'

One of Flora's cousins had enjoyed brief local fame, in Maybole, as Keith Grief, lead singer with the Kieftans.

Flora, lying on her sofa bed, with a packet of Marks and Spencer's cream cheese and chives crisps to hand, Mozart's Requiem playing quietly, dialled Aberdeen, picturing her father in a claret-coloured corduroy jacket which, in fact, his third wife had thrown out years before. He was on his fourth marriage now. Flora was the child of his second. When Flora had been a little girl, she had wanted to be a poet in a jacket with leather elbow patches. She had had her own study in the kneehole of Daddy's desk, where she had written her poems on a toy typewriter, but Daddy had left when she was five and her brother Hamish was three. Flora's third stepmother, Ishbel picked up the phone.

'Hello, Flora, how are you? Have you got snow down there too? What's the weather like?'

'Dreich,' said Flora. 'Foggy. A real mushroom-souper.'

'You'll be wanting a word with your father. Hang on, I'll give him a shout. He's just sorting out the boys' computers.'

'Don't bother,' Flora almost said, bitterly, but remembering that she was the bearer of bad news, forbore to hang up. Ishbel had taken to calling herself Bel since she had published her volume of verses on childbirth, *Drupes and Pomes*. Wedding photographs showed long brown hair cut in a fringe, under an Alice band of ice-blue roses, huge hazel eyes swimming behind hexagonal spectacles, dangling earrings, a gift from the groom, an outfit with too many lapels and a blue carnation in silver paper and a blouse with gilt-trimmed buttons the size of quails' eggs. The mail order catalogue bride, Ella had called her, but marriage had altered Ishbel. With all his faults, nobody could deny that George 'Dod' Loney was a worker, a grafter. That was what they said of him. He was a fanatical supporter of his football team, the Dons, and he had dreamed once of captaining Scotland in the Poetic League, so to speak. Now, here he is, turning out in all weathers for third-division fixtures, stiff-legged in his impeccable old-fashioned kit, bringing a whiff of brilliantine, starch and dubbin to the field of younger players, and the price tag for all those goalless draws, lost matches and substitutions could be read in the lines of his face. As if the usual fouls and penalties of literary life were not enough to contend with, Dod had a wife who was in greater demand on the poetry circuit than he was, a son who was making a name in the books pages of the English papers, and a daughter who was threatening to write a biography of a talent greater than himself, a profligate who had squandered his gifts, scored over and over again with an effortless arc of the ball from an impossible angle, and then been stretchered off in disgrace before half-time. Dod sucked on a bitter wedge of lemon.

Flora heard his feet on creaking stairs, loping up from the basement den, thought of the boys' computers and her tin

In shop windows all along the King's Road, pale spring clothes struck optimistic attitudes, gesturing behind wet glass to the people hurrying past in their winter black, with umbrellas blowing inside out and heads bowed against the February wind that came straight off the North Atlantic seaboard loaded with melting ice. Those pastel linens make you long for sunshine as yellow as the daffodils shivering on the flower stalls, Lily thought, for coral, sand, silver, turquoise, and spicy ochres bleached by the heat. She was on her way home from work, one of the crowd pouring in and out of Sloane Square tube station. Lily was seventeen and had just become aware of the importance of wearing colours appropriate to the seasons. She had only recently got the point of turquoise. True turquoise, not peacock blue or eau-de-nil or aquamarine or the debased hues of lacy bedjackets and babies' cardigans and velour leisure-suits that call themselves turquoise, but the vibrant stone of scarab and torque and misshapen ancient beads and Islamic glaze.

Pulling down the brim of the hat skewered to her rain-frizzled hair with a Bakelite pin in the shape of two Scottie dogs with rhinestone eyes, she quickened her pace, almost certain that tonight the letter would be waiting for her. She had to leave the house in Finchley, where she lived with her parents, before the post arrived in the morning, and it was tantalizing to think of that envelope lying on the hallstand all day, unopened. Surely the winner of the Untapped Talent Short Story Competition, sponsored by *Contour* magazine, with a first prize of two hundred pounds and guaranteed publication, must be notified soon.

Her story, 'Death by Art Deco', was gaudily painted, glittering and flamboyant, but would the judges appreciate that? Should she have made it more Fortuny and Arpège? As she passed the man selling the *Big Issue*, she was struck by the queasy thought that she ought to have mentioned the homeless. Or brought in drugs. Did a story about a serial killer have street cred now? She wished that she had taken the trouble to check out the judges, and read some of their work to see what they would go for. She had never even heard of two of them, but Andrea Heysham was famous. It was awesome to think of Andrea Heysham reading her story. Absorbed in that thought, Lily went through the ticket barrier and down the steps, and as she descended her conviction that her story was a winner rose again. Her job, as assistant to the miserable Welsh proprietors of Bizarre Bazaar, a tiny shop that specialized in jewellery and artefacts of the Twenties and Thirties, had proved inspirational in supplying authentic detail, and to avert the horror of Mr and Mrs Pritchard recognizing themselves in print as victims of the serial killer, she had turned them into a miserable Welsh gay couple, look you. There's cunning.

In a pink-washed terrace house not far from Sloane Square, Andrea Heysham was lying on the floor of her study surrounded by jiffy bags, paperclips, scrunched-up balls of paper and manuscripts. She had regretted agreeing to judge this competition as soon as the blasted stories arrived some weeks ago, hundreds of them it seemed, and now she could put off the disagreeable task no longer. She had to find her Untapped Talent tonight. Andrea was a tall woman in her late forties dressed in dusty black leggings and tunic that emphasized the top-heaviness they were meant to disguise. A fraught coronet of yellow hair stuck up in points from her working bandeau of black Lycra above her wide forehead, and a cigarette dropped ash. Reading glasses, resting on rounded cheekbones and a slightly retroussé nose, magnified her brown eyes. On the desk below the shelves of her own books in several languages – Andrea thought of herself as a dependable shrub which flowered every second summer – a wordprocessor sat in a plastic mac: wisely, for a coffee stain testified to the uncertain climate of the room. Andrea ought to have been working at it now, but the screen had been blank for weeks. Big coloured paperclips held wodges of unopened post and several invitations were stuck behind a bowl of sepia scentless rosebuds, fluff and cat fur, among the jumble of china and glass on the mantelpiece. Tarnished silver framed photographs of her parents, both dead now, and her son Kit's progression from beautiful babyhood through shining schooldays to handsome graduation. Kit was living somewhere in Camberwell now with a transpontine vampire called Melissa, wasting his education, not calling his mother, who found their estrangement almost unbearable. Andrea's elbow caught a glass of red wine, tipping it over the pages she was riffling through.

'Bugger.'

She ripped off a handful of sodden text and aimed it at an overflowing black bin liner. Pouring herself another drink, she read on for a couple of minutes before lobbing the remainder of it into the sack. An orange tabby cat came mewing in from the paved back garden out of the rain, running across the room to rub its wet back across her face. It left a trail of smudged pawprints across the papers.

'For goodness' sake, Pumpkin,' said Andrea, picking him up and kissing him, with the cigarette clamped in the side of her mouth. 'Those are somebody's dreams you're treading on.'

She crossed another name off her list and poured another drink. The haphazard pile of unread scripts was dwindling: any which contained the sentence 'That summer I sprouted breasts', or featured pubescent boys measuring their manhoods with school rulers went straight into the bin bag, along with half a dozen old clockmakers who had escaped the Nazis, all the homeless, a dozen giros, and several pounds of prize leeks and marrows. Andrea picked a cold baked bean from the transparent sleeve of 'Death by Art Deco' by Lily Richards, and ate it as she skimmed the pages. Pretty name, Lily.

'Pumpkin. I think we've found our winner!'

Good characterization. Those Welsh fairies, Dai and Dafydd, were remarkably like that ghastly couple at Bizarre Bazaar, who had overcharged her for a Lalique scent spray, some rather splendid earrings and a few bits and pieces of amusing tat. Neat plot too. Dai and Dafydd are poisoned by a rare Amazonian venom injected into matching pairs of faux pearl cufflinks. Andrea noted some minor critical points: 1. The opening sentence suggests a story about a ruthless serial killer yet the only victims are Dai (intentional pun?) and Dafydd. 2. Check spelling of Dafydd. Shd it be Dyffydd? 3. Writer has used the word 'faux' thirteen times.

Never mind, it would do. Now for two runners up. Andrea rooted around for three OK-looking manuscripts, the first of which turned out to be about a sensitive little boy who was rescued from his brutal stepfather by a talking dolphin. Then it was a toss up for third place between a peeping Tom and a woman who wrote poison-pen letters. Poison pen won on points because Pumpkin had plumped down on the penultimate page of peeping Tom, preventing Andrea from finishing it. She Tippexed a smear of cigarette ash from 'Boy with a Dolphin', wondering why men were so in love with themselves as little boys, and as she rose stiffly and slightly unsteadily to place her choices on her desk, red drops spattered them, from a finger cut on the sharp staple of a jiffy bag.

'Blood,' said Andrea. 'That's what they want, Pumpkin, blood.'

At the working lunch the following day the groomed and soignée public Andrea found herelf in fierce disagreement with her two fellow judges, both of whom had binned 'Death by Art Deco' as decisively as she had selected it. Swallowing her astonishment that they appeared to take the whole thing seriously, she felt it incumbent on her to champion her choice. The wispy Angelica Dodder favoured some account of a young girl's mental breakdown, which Andrea had missed. Well, as the author of *Mistletoe in a Dirty Glass*, a remaindered Virago Classic depicting her own descent into the netherworld, Angelica would, wouldn't she? Anybody could go into a loony bin and write about it, but that didn't make it Art: God knows Andrea had been tempted at times herself, and who didn't feel like cracking up at Christmas? It was only normal. Maldwyn Evans, with the tightly knotted tie, rimless glasses and neatly trimmed beard of the fanatic, agreed with Angelica and rejected 'Death by Art Deco' on political as well as aesthetic grounds.

'What do you mean, racist?' Andrea demanded, agitating an annoying thread of anchovy wound round a molar.

'It's anti-Welsh.'

'Don't be ridiculous. It's perfectly OK to hate the Welsh. They're white — well, white-ish. Everybody does.'

'I'm Welsh.'

'Oh, but I never think of you as Welsh, Maldwyn. I mean, you're not exactly Organ Morgan, are you?'

He flushed and pulled the knot of his tie even tighter. 'I'm sorry, Andrea. "Death by Art Deco" is disallowed by a majority decision, and that's final.'

'Well, screw you,' said Andrea and, turning to the waitress, demanded, 'Who snuck an anchovy on to this bruschetta?'

Angelica smiled placatingly at the waitress and looked anxiously from one to the other of the opponents, thrilled to be in a majority but fearful of unpleasantness. Why did everything always have to be spoiled? Andrea rounded on her, angrily projecting the image of the vampire Melissa on to their chosen winner. 'If you're determined to raise false hopes in the pierced breast of some tattooed neo-Goth with magenta dreadlocks and dirty fingernails poking out of torn lace gloves, on your own head be it. I resign.'

Her literary judgement had been questioned, that was what really rankled, and she had given up her time for free, for nothing. There was no way that she would admit now that her powers of discrimination might not have been quite up to par when she made her choice. She strode along the King's Road with an armful of scarlet amaryllis and a mouthful of chocolate; treats to console a hurt little girl, even if she had had to buy them herself. Andrea's longing to see Kit swelled and burst like bubblegum, leaving an empty hole as she noticed that the sun was shining on clouds like cold spring lambs. She went into Waitrose and bought a couple of little chops. Then, finding herself outside Bizarre Bazaar, she decided to put her bruised writer's instinct to the test. It was really only half a shop: the other side, which sold candles, was all purples and yellows and wafted the scent of wax lemons and violets and primroses over the cluttered shelves and glass cases of art deco true and faux.

A girl with eyes that were almost violet and a great bunch of hair the colour some call Titian, smiled at Andrea.

'Can I help you, or are you just browsing?'

'Browsing be buggered,' came a Welsh mutter. 'Sun's shinin', she's got wine on 'er breath, she's 'ad a good lunch, make a sale, girl! We done no bloody business all mornin'.'

Andrea looked round, at two heads bent over price lists, and back at the red-faced assistant. She had come to detest long hair, and you could make a coir doormat out of this lot, with enough left over for a set of coasters.

'I'm looking for something overpriced and preferably

fake,' she said. 'Something faux. No, actually, I think it might be you I've come to see. You're not by any chance Lily Richards, the writer, are you?'

'Oh my God,' Lily said. 'It's you, isn't it?'

'Lily, you've had your two warnings about social calls!' came the voice of Mr Pritchard again, before the girl could answer.

'Right then. I'll get my coat,' said Lily. 'Mr and Mrs Pritchard, you have just witnessed the beginning of my real life.'

Ten minutes later she was sitting opposite Andrea in Picasso's with a spoon of knickerbocker glory halfway to her quivering lips, and a big glacé cherry of grief stuck in her throat. Opposite Andrea Heysham, the famous novelist, who had come to seek her out only to half-break her heart.

'Do take your hair out of your ice cream.' Andrea took an irritated sip at her espresso. 'I've got a proposition to put to you.'

'It all sounds rather dubious, Lily,' her mother said, touching a petal of the amaryllis flaunting itself from a vase on the green oilcloth of their kitchen table, where she and Lily sat opposite each other. 'I never thought of these as cut flowers. You say she's offered you a job, but doing what, precisely? This Andrea Heysham may be a brilliant writer as you say,

57

but it's not as though you're a trained secretary, is it? I mean, you may not have liked the Pritchards, but at least that was a proper job.'

'Mum, I'm an amanuensis-cum-PA now, whether you like it or not!'

The strange word bloomed between them like one of the alien red lilies that woman had pressed on her gullible daughter. Janet Richards, who worked as a home help, blamed Lily's father, a telephone engineer who had fantasized about being a pop star until an audition for *New Faces* smashed his dreams, for not having backed her up in her bid to persuade Lily to go to college. She sat on at the table worrying after Lily left the kitchen. Writing was all very well as a hobby, she herself went to an art class once a week, but she couldn't see it as a career for a young girl with a handful of mediocre GCSEs. If she was serious in her ambition to be a writer, Lily should have applied herself at school and gone to university to study English. Janet accused a certain authoress too, whose name she had forgotten, who had come to Lily's school in her final term to run a series of creative writing workshops, putting ideas into Lily's head. She could have reminded Lily of that essay on *To Kill a Mockingbird* that she had got her dad to write for her, and in her conversation with Lily just now she had managed to bite back the truth, that Lily's story had actually been rejected. She had seen Andrea Heysham's books in the library but had somehow never got round to taking one out. Now she almost hated her, as if Andrea Heysham were trying to take her daughter away from her. The Chelsea Set, she thought, her lips pursed in a sneer.

Lily, who that afternoon had seen her hopes and ambitions melting in a tall glass, only to be reglorified by Andrea, went out to the hall to telephone her boyfriend through a blur of disappointed tears. In the silence that followed her news she picked a nodule of paint from her mother's 'View of Finchley Rooftops' that hung above the phone. Then he said, 'You want to watch out. She probably fancies you. You know what those literary types are like.'

'If that's what you think, Damian, I've nothing further to say to you.'

Janet's doubts would have been confirmed if Lily had told her that she had spent her first morning in her new job taking Pumpkin to the vet for his booster flu jab, and part of the afternoon shopping in Marks and Spencer for Andrea's dinner party. Lily kept her fingers crossed that she would be invited to stay and meet some of Andrea's writer friends, as she was a literary type herself now, but after she had Hoovered and dusted and polished the drawing room Andrea told her she could go home. She was between cleaners, she explained, and had been too busy to do any housework for a couple of weeks.

'Is this your son?' Lily asked, picking up Kit's graduation photograph in its shining silver frame. 'He's really good-looking, isn't he? What's he doing now?'

'Shacking up with some troglodyte south of the river,' replied Andrea. 'You know where the dusters and things live, don't you?' Lily's snubbed look reminded her of the job description she had concocted.

'We'll make a start on some of the backlog of post tomorrow,' she promised.

Lily sat in her bedroom with a notebook at the white melamine child's desk Dad had got her from MFI years ago and made a start on her novel, *True Turquoise*. Mum's voice came from the hall.

'Who's picked the smoke off my chimney? Lily, don't you want to watch *Brookside*?'

'*Brookside* schmookside!' said Lily.

She wished she were in a room in Chelsea with paintings by real artists on the yellow walls and an iridescent classical CD spinning round, at work on a word processor, with a drinkypoo at hand. That was what Andrea had called her lunchtime Bloody Mary, using invisible inverted commas to indicate irony.

At one o'clock in the morning Andrea started clearing plates in a half-hearted way.

'You should get a dishwasher, Andrea,' her best friend remarked, taking the hint to ring for a cab.

'I have,' said Andrea. 'In a manner of speaking.'

After they had all gone Andrea sat on, smoking, thinking about Lily. Admittedly, pique at Angelica and Maldwyn had prompted her to tell the girl that she had chosen her story, but some impulse had made her take Lily on. It wasn't just because her latest cleaning lady had walked out. Perhaps, unconsciously, she had planned to replace Kit's Gothic girlfriend with an untainted flower. Was she then a procuress manqué? Why was she so unhappy? She had success, even if it meant people making all sorts of demands, all take and no give; she had Pumpkin, her friends, her house; she could afford to travel, but she was finding it increasingly difficult to motivate herself, with only the cat to turn to for advice, to make her feel real. Having Lily around would avert the danger of becoming a recluse, she thought, with her roots growing out until her hair looked like burnt toast spread with margarine, and of being found dead one day beneath an avalanche of paper, while the answerphone exploded with piled-up messages.

Andrea tried to be positive: she knew she would get Kit back again. Nothing could break that bond. And she genuinely liked Lily, who reminded her a little of herself when young, before her genius had turned out to be a middle-brow talent. But in admitting Lily to her life she would make herself vulnerable by exposing the reality of it, so different from the dreams of a starstruck amateur. She knew so much about so many things: mother love, love, the deaths of parents, of friends, divorce. She had lived so long that her work should have achieved the profound stateliness of a mature symphony, and yet she had nothing to say. It was out of the question that she would fail to deliver on time, but at this rate she would soon be reduced to dashing off a novel set in Chelsea, about a novelist with writer's block. Perhaps she should get out of town for a bit and bring back a sack of fertilizer for her imagination.

Kit Heysham was lying awake beside Melissa, who was curled up with her face to the wall. Moonlight and streetlight diffused by the cotton bedspread tacked over the window glittered on the crystals suspended on threads from the ceiling. Melissa had taken them from Phantasmagorica, the shop in Covent Garden where she had worked until recently. He heard her mutter in her sleep, the swooping sound of police cars, the tap in the shared kitchen dripping, the nocturnal sounds of a decaying house in multiple occupation, and shifted his position carefully, negotiating the wire sticking through the mattress. He thought about his mother. He hadn't read any of her books but he had witnessed enough of her hard work to respect her for them, even if he *had* sold her typewriter when he was nine years old.

His father had married again and although Kit quite liked his half-sisters, he didn't visit very often. His mother and stepmother had something in common, besides Dad, Kit thought bitterly; both of them had been horrible to Melissa when they'd met her. He decided to take her round to Mum's again, if he could persuade her, so that Andrea could see how wrong she had been. He wanted them to be friends. Trying to get comfortable, he pulled the rubber band painfully from his ponytail and let his hair fan loose over his bare shoulders, releasing its vapours into the night air. It would be nice to have a bath at Mum's too.

'There's no way I'm going round there to be insulted,' said Melissa in the morning when he suggested calling on Andrea. 'Snobby cow.'

'We could have a bath there, she wouldn't mind,' he cajoled her.

'Yes she would. What's wrong with our bathroom here, if you're so keen on the idea?'

'It's filthy, and it's not really our bathroom, is it?'

'Oh, poor little Kitty, does he want his own bathroom den? I thought public school was meant to make you tough and enjoy bathing in other people's dirty bathwater?'

'It was only a very minor public school.'

'What's she call you Kit for, anyway? Why couldn't she just call you Chris like anybody else?'

The visit to Andrea's was deferred.

Like a child with a new best doll, Andrea started to take Lily about with her. Dressed in ice-cream colours, they went shopping, to a couple of private views and a few publishing parties. People began to speculate whether they were an item. Andrea also introduced Lily to her hairdresser, and the annoying mass of hair slithered to the floor in a heap of snakes. Lily's mother cried when she saw the result, but had to concede that it showed off Lily's cheekbones. Her father said he supposed it would grow back for the winter and asked how much it had cost, and Lily, who had no idea, had to lie, and then she felt guilty. The whole atmosphere of the house was upset by her new look. Meanwhile, *True Turquoise* almost filled two notebooks; admittedly, she hadn't managed to work in any turquoise yet, but Andrea had approved of the title. She was going to put it on Andrea's wordprocessor when it was finished. 'Death by Art Deco' she filed away, for the collection of stories which would follow the novel. It was so brilliant having Andrea to advise her; the only thing was, Andrea herself never seemed to write anything, even though she was always dressed in her writing outfit of leggings, tunic and headband when Lily arrived in the morning. She spent much of her time talking on the telephone, reading and going out to lunch and the opera or the theatre. 'I'm working in my head all the time,' she explained when Lily plucked up the courage to voice her fear that the next addition to Andrea's oeuvre might be late in delivery. 'And in my dreams. Putting words on paper is the easy part. Don't you find?'

'Oh, yes!' Lily agreed.

Each morning Lily, as amanuensis, had to deal with the quantities of post which came through Andrea's door. 'Refuse all requests to perform for nothing and bin anything upsetting from charities, everything from charities, in fact,' Andrea had instructed, 'and brown envelopes addressed in purple, green or red biro. They are from loonies and shouldn't be opened. Just use your initiative and get rid of anything that looks dreary or claims to be from somebody I was at school with. Manuscripts, and they are without exception unsolicited, come under that heading, and first novels hoping for a quote, unless you want them yourself. Vet the fan letters and give me only those that really merit a reply. I'll give you a list of the people I'm in to on the telephone. Oh, and tell any students writing theses to do their own bloody research, that's what they get grants for.'

Lily felt honoured at being asked to protect Andrea from all those awful people. She bought herself a stretchy working bandeau like Andrea's, even though her hair was too short to need one, and found it really helped. She was reading her way through Andrea's books, which were as brilliant as she had expected. Her admiration was soured only by jealousy of the characters who had lived in Andrea's head and heart, especially the girls, and she scrutinized herself anxiously for any of the faults which Andrea had criticized. It seemed that she had little in common with any of her friends now. She asked her mother to do bagels with cream cheese and scallions for breakfast, and she took up smoking at work and learned to enjoy a weak Bloody Mary. Andrea was getting through at least a hundred cigarettes a day. 'Why does that blasted son of mine never ring?' she growled. Kit must be mad, Lily thought: if she had a mother like Andrea, she'd be round there all the time.

'I've decided to go away for the weekend,' Andrea told her one Friday morning. 'To some friends in the country. Pick up some local colour, sort of thing. Do you think you could possibly –'

'Babysit Pumpkin? Yes of course. I'd love to! You have a nice break, you really deserve one.'

On the Saturday morning, Kit let himself and Melissa into the house. They could hear a Hoover upstairs.

'Mum?' he called.

There was no answer, and he led the way up to the study. The sound of the Hoover died. Kit pushed open the door and someone sprang across the room at him with a dagger.

Melissa screamed. He grabbed a wrist, and saw it belonged to a mad-looking girl with her hair sticking out of a black band, clutching a silver paperknife.

'What are you doing here? Why are you wearing my mother's headband?'

'You're Kit, aren't you? I'm sorry. I thought you were a burglar.'

He let go of her.

'Who are you? Does my mother know you're here?'

'I'm Andrea's amanuensis. Lily.'

'What?'

'She's the cleaner, Chris!' said Melissa. 'What a crap job.'

'I recognized you from your photos,' Lily told Kit, ignoring Melissa. 'Your mother's really upset that you haven't been in touch. She'll be devastated to have missed you.'

She tried to smile at him, but they were intruders in the yellow room that now belonged to her and Andrea. They smelled of – mildew and Camel cigarettes, and Melissa, who looked like something malevolent from beyond the grave, with several silver rings in each ear, one long purple glass teardrop, and two rings in her nose, had picked up a Victorian figurine and was examining her lacy porcelain drawers with a tattooed talon.

'Yeah, well,' said Kit, 'we haven't got a phone, and you know how it is with call boxes, all vandalized or out of order when you want one.'

'Not any more,' said Lily. 'My father's a telephone engineer and he says that –'

'Where is my mother, anyway?' Kit interrupted her.

'She's gone to the country for the weekend, to see some friends.'

'Typical,' said Melissa. 'Well, might as well have a bath since we've come all this way.'

'Would you like some coffee?' Lily asked Kit when Melissa had gone. She remembered that she wanted to make friends with him, to be the one who brought him and Andrea together again. She tried not to mind his unwashed hair, fair like Andrea's but dull with the grease of a hundred burgers and chips.

'I'll make it. Mustn't keep you from your work.'

Kit was deflated and disappointed, and he had bribed Melissa needlessly.

He picked up the Hoover hose and handed it to Lily with a courteous, distancing smile and left the room, with the treacherous Pumpkin squawking at his heels. Lily burst into tears.

'I'm not the bloody cleaner. I'm a writer!'

To think she had often secretly fantasized about sitting round the kitchen table with Kit and Andrea, like a family, Melissa having been dumped.

It took her ages to clear up the kitchen after they had gone, and she had to remove a sickening nest of brown and magenta hairs from the plughole of the bath, in a piece of loo paper, with her eyes closed, and flush the toilet twice before it disappeared. Then she found a note from Kit to his mother on Andrea's desk, giving his address. 'Love ya, Mels' was scrawled across the bottom. Lily, still feeling violated and diminished by them, and sick after disposing of their hair, ripped the note furiously into little pieces and then, horrified at what she had done, hid the evidence under the debris of their lunch in the bin.

'You look terrible,' said Andrea on her return, dripping bluebells and red campion and cowparsley. 'Has anything happened to Pumpkin?'

'No, no, he's fine. Good as gold. I just don't feel very well. I think I'd better go home.'

Andrea felt cheated of her homecoming, but said, 'Poor baby. OK then, off you go. Take a cab. I've had a wonderful time. Can't wait to get down to some work, actually, you'll be delighted to hear, and I've got lots of plans for tubs for the garden. We can go plant shopping tomorrow, when you're feeling better.'

For three days Lily lay in bed, listlessly watching soaps on the little portable television with her own guilty drama playing in her head, and sleeping fitfully while a film of dust formed on the Lucozade her mother brought each morning before she left for work. Andrea might never see Kit again, and all because of her. In her dreams, she found Kit's note, restored, and Andrea threw her arms round her and hugged and kissed her. Lily woke in tears, sweating in the sunshine assaulting her through the window. She made desperate plans to haunt Camberwell until she ran into Kit, so that she could explain that the note had been sucked into the vacuum cleaner and then beg him to ring Andrea, without mentioning his visit. She would do anything he asked in return. But how could she find him? There wasn't even a tube station in Camberwell where she could lurk. *True Turquoise* lay untouched under her bed. On the fourth day she got dressed, but it was even worse wandering round the small house like a tormented ghost. How could she have done that to Andrea? How could she have been such a spiteful, jealous coward? Andrea would hate her when she found out. What lies could she tell her to make her go on liking her? Her mother had telephoned Andrea for her, to explain that Lily was suffering from a nasty bug, and had been won over by Andrea's warm concern for Lily. Pumpkin sent a funny Get Well postcard. Lily could hardly look at it.

After a week Lily, faint with apprehension, rang the Chelsea doorbell. Andrea let her into a house smelling of bluebells gone bad, kissing her on the cheek for the first time. Lily recoiled, unworthy, remembering her dreams.

'Sorry, I am a bit garlicky. Had people round last night. I'm afraid we've left a bit of a mess. Come and have some coffee. Do you feel up to a bit of gardening? This weather's too divine to waste, isn't it? I've managed to get quite a bit of work done this last week too – it hasn't been all partying. You're shivering! That d. and v. really takes it out of you, doesn't it?'

Lily felt unable to thank Pumpkin for his postcard. She piled up dirty plates in a silent miserable confusion of wanting to confess and terror of the consequences, while Andrea opened a fresh jar of coffee. She plunged the spoon through the foil with a crack that made Lily jump.

'By the way, Lily –'

Lily's heart lurched. Andrea knew of her crime.

Andrea kept her back to Lily, spooning coffee into two mugs, keeping it casual.

'Have you got my earrings?'

'Earrings?'

Relief, then a new panic, left Lily hot and cold. The kettle boiled and switched itself off. Andrea turned round, and saw guilt written all over Lily's face.

'The dangly black Bakelite ones, with faux pearls? I don't mind you borrowing my things, only I wish you'd ask. They are rather precious to me, and worth a bit and I would like them back.'

Andrea, picturing the naked branch of the little velvet tree where the earrings should have hung, and remembering her search for them, and the shocking realization that they had been taken, nevertheless was still hoping that the matter could be settled without further embarrassment.

'I never touched your personal things,' said Lily. 'Any of them. I wouldn't! I've got too much respect.'

'Look, Lily, there's no point in prolonging this. We both know you did, so why not just say so?'

'But I didn't. I didn't! You can't say I did. You must have lost them yourself, in a taxi or somewhere, without noticing at the time. You often lose things when you've been — when you've been out. You know you do.'

At that Andrea wanted to slap the lies and defiance off Lily's white, tearful face. She felt a fool for having missed her. Her plans for the garden were collapsing in a stupid heap of compost. That silly postcard she'd sent from the cat.

'Oh, come on,' she said. 'I told you I don't mind. Just put them back and we'll forget the whole thing.'

Put them back. Like a thief.

'You've got to believe me. I swear I never touched your earrings.'

Lily stared back at an Andrea turned ugly, with no make-up and little puckers of skin under her eyes, arms folded across her enormous cat-furred chest, and a voice gone hard and posher, as if she were accusing a servant.

'This is ridiculous,' came out of thick pale lips like the

rind of ham. 'I was willing to turn a blind eye to the fact that you helped yourself to most of my vodka and my bath oil, but this has gone too far!'

'Melissa!' Revelation flooded over Lily. 'Melissa took them! It must have been Melissa! They were here, her and Kit, while you were away. It must have been her. She had a bath. They both did. And they were drinking vodka!'

Andrea screwed up her eyes to shut out the image of Kit and Melissa splashing about in scented oil in her bath, glugging vodka from the bottle.

'How can you stand there, in my kitchen, telling such disgusting lies? How dare you use my son to manufacture an alibi to get yourself off the hook? If Kit was here, where's his note? I know my own son, he would at least have left a note. How could you be so cruel?'

'I'm not cruel.' Lily sobbed.

'No? What about that story you wrote, ridiculing your employers, wasn't that cruel? You betrayed them as you have betrayed me. I expect I'll be your next victim. Grist to your mill.'

'Kit did leave a note.'

'Oh yes? Where is it then? Why didn't you give it to me?'

'I – I – forgot.'

'You forgot,' Andrea repeated heavily. 'My only son who I haven't seen for months just happens to turn up the one weekend I'm away and leaves me a note, and you "forgot" to give it to me. How very convenient. I suppose you'll come up with some cock-and-bull story about Pumpkin eating it next. And putting the blame on poor little Melissa. How *low* of you, Lily.'

Her chin quivered into a pitted lemon and crumpled. Tears spurted from her eyes and she wiped her hand across her nose, giving a choking snort. 'First Kit and now you.'

At seeing Andrea broken, by her, and in the impossibility of saying anything at all, Lily picked up her bag and started backing through the door.

'Yes, go!' Andrea was shouting. 'Go! Get out of my house! And those earrings had better be in tomorrow's post or we'll see what your mother has to say! My friends warned me against you. "Remember that film *All About Eve*," they said. My God, I wish I'd listened to them. And your racist little story wasn't up to much anyway. Did you know you'd used the word "faux" thirteen times? Is that the mark of a writer? Is it? And serial killers are of no interest whatsoever, not that yours was too successful with only two victims, was he? They're old hat, stale buns, nerds in elastic-waisted anoraks! How many serial killers have *you* met? Your story's phoney, fake. It's all false, false, false, like you, Lily Richards! Faux faux faux faux faux faux …'

Lily rushes out into the glare of the street, groping blindly in her bag as she runs, flinging her writing bandeau away in a black circle that loops the aerial of a passing car. Then she is

74

running along the King's Road, bashing into people, in the glitter and noise, streaked with the shame of her writing, her life, her whole self that Andrea had torn into pieces and dumped like garbage from a bin over her head, running until an insurmountable barrier of loss suddenly slams down ahead of her and she stops abruptly in the middle of the pavement, knocking an ice cream out of a child's hand.

The Wilderness Club

When there was such a glut of travel writers that they were piled in bleaching bales on quaysides all over the world, and traders in souks and bazaars couldn't give them away, even with an ounce of rhino horn or a kilo of ugli fruit thrown in, it was hardly surprising that Romney's disappearance went unnoticed.

It was Tusker Laidlaw, at a loss for an anecdote with which to bore the company at Romney's London club, the Wilderness, who remarked that nobody had heard a dicky bird from young Tiny Romney since he had departed for a small archipelago off the coast of West Africa. The members consulted the globe, but, curiously, could not locate the islands. Theirs was a claret and gravy-coloured world, but even when they had rung for old Shell to bring a damp cloth and he had exposed enough blue ocean to make a pair of sailor's trousers, there could be no doubt that the islands had vanished.

"Straordinary thing,' said Laidlaw. 'Reminds me of a tale I heard of the madam of a house of ill-repute in Marsails. Came from Dulwich, of all places, or was it Dunstable ...'

So exclusive was the Wilderness that its members were obliged under the rules to take turns as Club Bore, and

Tusker took his duties seriously. Age had sprinkled salt and pepper on the crumbs of ancient Stilton and twists of biltong in his mane of hair and full beard; he was gaunt and concave in his safari suit, and the upper of his scaly left shoe had disengaged from its sole, exposing a set of pointed yellow teeth. He bored on manfully, one of an endangered species, for where was the glamour of these old hunters now that hoi polloi could gorge on boil-in-the-bag ostrich from the Surrey veldt?

As Tusker bored on, a young woman named Clover Jones, wearing a borrowed Paul Smith suit, clenched her lovely jaw as the newspaper's fashion and beauty department stippled stubble on her ivory skin and jelled back her newly cropped black hair. Clover's brief was to penetrate the Wilderness, whose portals no woman had ever breached. A better journalist than she had bluffed her way into certain male preserves, but this was Clover's big challenge. Gossip columnists had dubbed her 'the Zuleika Dobson *de nos jours*', and she was determined to prove herself as a writer.

A quick snort in the Ladies, a gulp of mineral water, and Clover clamped on her hat, adjusted the Versace sunglasses that could not dim the radiance of her eyes, and strode out to impersonate a long-lost nephew of one Typhoon Tucker, an old India hand. Or was it Typhoo? She ignored the burst of unkind laughter behind her; it was hardly her fault that her father was the paper's star columnist. They'd laugh on the other side of their faces when she was Literary Editor. She just wished she were better briefed to converse with the old buffer. If only she'd taken O-level geography, but it was not her fault she'd been asked to leave her boarding school. By the other girls.

Her initial ploy had been to write to Tusker Laidlaw, posing as a would-be biographer, but he had smelled a rat, as the remaindered copies of his memoirs suggested that no publisher would touch him with a bargepole. A researcher had spent days in the cuttings library before coming up with any Wildernessers at all for Clover. Waiting for a taxi, she concentrated her mind: brinjal, she remembered, bhaji, Bhageera, that's Indian for panther, Shere Hite, no, Khan, tiger; Kaa, a snake; Baloo a bear, and King Louis, he's the king of the swingers, a Jungle VIP …

And as Tusker still bored on, 'young' Tiny Romney was lolling in the back of a taxi stuck in traffic, in a cacophony of car hooters and police sirens.

'I do not believe it!' the taxi driver kept repeating. 'One minute bleeding Marble Arch is there, the next it's gone! One minute it's standing there minding its own business, the next – Wham! Gone! I don't believe it!'

'When you've seen as much of the world as I have, my friend,' said Romney wearily, suppressing a belch, 'you'll believe anything.'

Sharp, heavy pains racked him as masonry shifted inside

him. He was heading for the ugliest place he could imagine, his club. There was nowhere else for him to go. The driver stared at his passenger. Big when he had boarded, now in his striped djellaba he seemed to fill the cab. Rivers of sweat gushed from his huge forehead, splashed his dark glasses and coursed down his marble-white cheeks. Grinding noises came from the vast stomach. Suppose he was a pregnant woman in disguise, taking advantage of our NHS, about to give birth? To a baby the size of an elephant. With Muggins acting as midwife.

'Not in my cab, you don't,' he started to say, but the traffic began to move and he was forced to drive on. A look in the mirror showed no movement from chummy, who even seemed to have shrunk a little.

There were those who said that Romney was as camp as a row of tents, others who retorted that he *was* a row of tents, or at least a marquee, while some swore that no woman was safe in his company. None of them was entirely right. Romney was an omnivore.

Clover Jones had once written a feature on 'Men Who Love Too Much' (it had to be spiked: all her interviewees fell in love with her), but had not encountered a single example of the rare syndrome from which Romney suffered. Documented case histories were few; in England there was the man with an orchestra inside him, and a woman who had ingested Hampstead Garden Suburb in blossom time. Her story ended in tragedy after a trip to the bulb fields of Holland, and the post-mortem revealed advanced botanical hyperaesthesia and an abnormally receptive nervous system. The pathologist was able to return a missing giant water lily to Kew.

Romney's agony abated as Marble Arch diminished and settled under his heart. He cursed himself. He had fled England because he wanted to preserve it, and within an hour of his return he had eaten part of its heritage. It was not even his favourite monument. He had risked removing his shades for a second, and with the nostalgic recognition had come the dreaded intake of breath, the burning salt breaker of tears, the racing pulse. Then the uncontrollable suction, and the edifice embedded in his innards.

London, on an evening on the verge of spring, was the most dangerous place for Romney, but what could he do? He had fallen in love with the lush islands of his exile, and, bloated with them, he had floated back to the mainland. What had he to look forward to? He dared not visit the opera or ballet or any art gallery, and as for human contact – he shuddered at the thought of the near-miss before Marble Arch had left a crater in the road. He had glimpsed, darkly, a lighted upper window, a paper lampshade printed with the globe, bunk beds, a jumbled pinboard, two children's heads. Just in time, a parental hand had pulled down the blind.

Like Clover's, his academic career had been cut short,

when early signs of the disease were manifest. As a small chorister he had sobbed so loudly at the other boys' pure trebles that he had to be removed from the chapel, and he was stretchered off the field at the inter-house match although he had only been a spectator. His last school report had read: 'Romney, alas, is entirely lacking in the gaiety and innocence and heartlessness which we look for in our boys.'

Now he knew himself condemned to live out his life in the twilight of the Wilderness Club, to take his turn as the Bore, to watch Tusker Laidlaw spooning quince jelly on to his suppertime bone. He would cultivate the mushrooms and ferns of the dank, tiled bathrooms, and while away the aching hours in the library, devouring its mildewed books. And when that all became too much to bear, there were the assegais to fall back on.

Clover paid off her cab, turning down the driver's offer to take her to Madame Jojo's later. God, it wasn't fair! Even dressed as a bloke! She remembered seeking refuge from her beauty's impact in a convent retreat. On her way home to inform her parents of her new-found Vocation, she had been rudely awoken from a reverie of wimples by the sight of Reverend Mother and Sister Anthony pelting after the bus.

Now a bitter wind blew away her courage and flimsy pretext. Sick with fear, she hovered near the club's entrance. Then she saw her chance. A huge striped figure was mounting the steps. As the heavy door opened, Clover hurled herself forward, to catch hold of its skirts and be pulled inside.

She tripped and crashed on to hard mosaic, hitting her head on the corner of a glass case. Lying in the brownish gloom, she was aware of spears and snarling heads on the walls and woozily recalled the rumour that to be blackballed at the Wilderness was to be shot, and as the mummified creature in the glass case swam into focus Clover wondered if she were indeed the first woman to cross this threshold. Then the great striped person was lifting her tenderly, propping her up. Simultaneously, automatically, they raised a hand to remove their dark glasses.

Trouser Ladies

One by one the pumpkins, heavy orange lamps glowing against the deepening blue dusk, are carried into the shop and extinguished. Oranges, lemons, satsumas, pomegranates follow in procession, and when the greengrocer's grass, bleached now by the street lights, is rolled up in a strip of muddy turf, the woman watching from her window turns away into her own life in a room lit by tangerine glass globes and fans. A low band of sound runs past her like a pattern etched into the glass, a dado on the wallpaper, so familiar that she hasn't heard it for years and, besides, Beatrice at seventy-six is becoming a little deaf. Her white hair is still thick, while the embroidered kimono she is wearing, for she is in the process of getting ready to go out, has faded from peacock to azure and worn to patches of gossamer grids and loose hammocks of threads slung between blossoms and birds. She has let herself be diverted by the street because she is apprehensive about the evening, fearing that it will be an uneasy walk down a memory lane signposted by someone else's reminiscences, made strange like a road in a dream. As a journalist she had been photographed in battledress and safari suit in theatres of war, but she is in a blue funk at the thought of meeting the daughter of her best and dearest, now dead, friend in the neutral territory of a restaurant.

Catriona Ling had seen the announcement of Beatrice Alloway's birthday in the paper, had telephoned her, and was probably regretting her impulse as much as Beatrice rued her surprised acceptance.

Chinese lanterns and bronze and yellow chrysanthemums, birthday tokens, are crammed into a Bizarre jug on a low table and a glass rectangle in front of the tiny black grate-basket; and on the mantelpiece, at the centre of a jumble of cards and invitations, is a branch of spindle-berries in a conical blue vase. Beatrice bought them herself, making her birthday the excuse for extravagance. They cost her six pounds, but she had to have them. She catches her breath each time she sees the pinkish-red four-lobed fruits opening in the warmth of the room like a flight of wing-cases across the cobalt-blue wall, flaunting their orange seeds. One of her birthday cards, the one from Catriona's twin sisters, had cast a blight of unease over her birthday, and although it is hidden by another card, it obtrudes as she gazes at the spray of spindle and remembers Betty's excitement when they came upon a spindle tree, the first either of them had seen, at the edge of a little wood in Kent more than forty years ago.

It had been the afternoon of Beatrice's ill-conceived visit to Canterbury. What she had hoped or imagined would come from a descent on Betty's domesticity she did not know then and couldn't say now, just that she had been overcome by longing to see her again. Beatrice Alloway and

Betty Gemmell had grown up together in Ardrossan, gone to school and university together, and then Betty had married Alec Ling, the boy next door. Betty and Alec, and their son, wee Donald, went to London to seek their fortune, found that the streets were not paved with gold, and now Alec was a miner, digging away in the Kent coalfield to support a growing family. Beatrice's unannounced arrival that Sunday had caused a confusion that had sent them all, Alec, Betty, Donald, the twins Heather and Erica and four-year-old Catriona out on this awkward walk. Suddenly there was the spindle tree, exotic and English, with red leaves and pink fruit trembling on delicate stalks in the blue autumn sky. Heather and Erica held up the baby dolls Beatrice had brought, to admire the berries, and Beatrice wished that the whole lot of them, Alec and the children, would prick their fingers on a spindle and fall asleep, like the Sleeping Beauty's court, so that she and Betty could be alone together.

Then, like the good sport she was, Auntie Bee was instigating a game of hide-and-seek, whooping through falling leaves, bobbing up behind bushes and letting the children pelt her with damp handfuls of red and brown and yellow, chasing them round tree trunks.

The smell of kicked-up leaves, fungus and lichen is pungent in her head as she opens her wardrobe and takes out the black suit in which she will face the evening. The trouble

91

was, and is, Betty Gemmell was the love of her life, and she was Betty's best friend.

Ting-a-ling-ling goes the old-fashioned black bell on the shop door, saying our names because it belongs to us, the Ling twins, Heather and Erica, Erica and Heather — our names were Father's little joke. He loved all the *Ericaceae*, and sprinkled sand on our cloddy garden to make them feel at home. When we moved into our brand-new council house in Canterbury, all the gardens were raw, shining clay; like everybody else, we planted vegetables and chrysanthemums and Esther Reeds, big white daisies or marguerites that we children took to harvest festival in the firm, solid bunches with a blob of carnations at the centre like the jam on semolina, but only Father grew heathers and dwarf conifers in crazy paving. Mother preferred heather growing wild, in Scotland, where our family came from. She hated dwarf conifers.

We had come down south in 1948, first to dismal lodgings where we were all very unhappy, and then to our new house, east of the Martyr's Memorial, near a railway bridge where you could stand and let the trains puff great cornets of pink and white steam and smoke over you so that it was like being at the heart of an ice cream. Canterbury had been badly bombed in the war, and when you were out playing you came on half-houses, with staircases leading nowhere, rising from the rubble of buddleia, willowherb and toadflax, smashed bricks and glass and porcelain, and rolls of brambles and barbed wire. You squeezed through the corrugated iron that fenced off the wasteland and found heaps of jagged slates for tomahawks lying among the nettles, and once a gang of us discovered a shining pile of aluminium offcuts that made swords and arrows beyond our wildest dreams. A boy called Goldfish was shot in the tongue, but lived to tell the tale.

Of course, it's all changed a lot now, but we can still see it as it was, the streets of little houses behind privet hedges and hydrangeas, with beds visible in front rooms, and old men with two sticks sitting on walls, and people limping along on one big black surgical boot, with a steel stirrup to make their legs the same length. And even now one of us just has to say 'Remember' and the smell of our house comes back in whiffs of pastel distemper, bright patterned carpet, the new wood and varnish of the furniture smelling like Lefevre's, where we bought it, and the ploughed earth of the garden glittering with bits of bottle glass, fragments of pottery and oyster shells.

We can remember school too, vividly, and it's quite strange when one of our old schoolmates comes into the shop accompanied by children or grandchildren, but mostly we get tourists. Our little shop is near the cathedral and we sell pretty things, angels and illustrated bibles, silver Canterbury crosses and Celtic jewellery, cards, bookmarks, gargoyles and so forth, and we live in the flat above, overlooking the River Stour and the Westgate Towers and gardens. It seems as though people don't really change, they just grow bigger, and when some middle-aged voice asks for this or that, they might as well be saying, 'Got any fag cards, twin?'

We had. Fat bundles of them, in rubber bands.

'Got any film stars? Who's your favourite film star, twin?'

Doris Day, we said. We hadn't seen any of her films, but you had to have a favourite film star. Some children queued up after the register for National Savings stamps with pictures of Prince Charles and Princess Anne, and had scrapbooks of the royal family. Our brother Donald belonged to a stamp club, Catriona collected bits of coloured glass which she called her jewels, and woolly caterpillars whom she called her friends; and we latched on to Doris Day. One day our made-up love for her became real. Mother's best friend Beatrice, whom we always called Auntie Bee, although we hadn't met her and we only knew her from the Christmas presents she sent us, was a journalist and sometimes she sent Mother magazines and we would fall on them with our blunt scissors in the hopes of finding a picture of Doris Day inside. Pink and white, gingham and golden, laughing eyes as blue as speedwells or periwinkles, with her wide, eager, cream-cheese smile, Doris Day was our goddess. Not an ideal to aspire to, for we knew that we, with our ginger hair and scratched legs and floppy cotton socks, hadn't a hope of growing into anything resembling Doris.

Film stars were an entirely different species then, a race apart; we couldn't tell one from another of this current lot if we wanted to, no grace, no style, no glamour, no charm, no charisma, no quality, and we're still waiting for the real film stars to come back, to descend from Valhalla and reclaim Hollywood.

It must have been about 1951, the year of the Festival of Britain, when we finally got to meet Auntie Bee. At that time, women wearing trousers were a comparatively rare sight, apart from bus conductresses and the occasional brown landgirl in a brown landscape, glimpsed through a bus window. Catriona used to call them 'trouser ladies'. It was a dull autumn Sunday afternoon, and we were sitting reading on the windowsill of our front room, Heather sitting on the left as usual, Erica on the right-hand side and Catriona was standing in the middle, on the little sea-grass stool, when suddenly she said, 'Here comes a trouser lady. And she's coming to our house!'

It was true. A trouser lady was coming up our path. She was in our porch, knocking at our door.

'Beatrice! What a wonderful surprise! I can't believe it's really you!' Mother was laughing and almost crying, hugging the trouser lady. 'Children, this is your Auntie Bee, at long last!'

'Let me look at you all!' said Auntie Bee. 'Donald, Heather, Erica, Catriona! They've all got your red hair, Betty! Alec, hello!'

'Just the one bag, Beatrice?' said Father. 'I do hope that this doesn't mean you're not planning a good long stay with us?'

A cold shiver ran through us. Father was smiling, but only the family could tell when he was just pretending to be nice, and sometimes even we got it wrong.

'Come away in, pet,' he said. Something had made him cross; perhaps it was that Bee had said we all had Mother's hair.

'Dad's got red hair too,' said Donald. His own was dark red like Father's; Mother's, ours and Catriona's was fiery and crinkly and leapt and sparked at the hairbrush's strokes. We were always losing our ribbons and Kirbygrips.

Bee had brought us all presents; Meccano for Donald, a teddy bear for Catriona, and twin dolls for us. They were delicate featured, with rosebud mouths and blue eyes that opened and closed, and feathery painted light brown hair. One of them had a soft green knitted dress and bonnet tied with ribbons, the other was dressed in lavender blue. We called them Suzannah and Maria. They were very pale, and when we took them to the baby clinic – Jamie was born about nine months after Bee's visit – the nurse weighed Suzannah and Maria and told us to give them more porridge. We did.

Auntie Bee stayed for five days, and we would race home from school at dinner time and in the afternoon to see her, and she would let us all get into her bed when we took her a cup of tea in the morning. The only thing that spoiled it was Father. He was in a bad mood all the time and argued continuously with Bee. If she had said the coal was black, he would have sworn it was white. One teatime he threw his food at the wall and he hit Donald around the head for spilling his milk. The trouble was, Bee didn't know that you had to agree with everything Father said.

Bee tried to put things right. 'Let's all go to the pictures,' she said. At that Father stormed out to the lodge – which was what everybody used to call the big garden sheds – and Mother couldn't come because Catriona was too little. So Bee and Donald and we two set out. It was thrilling; we had never been to the cinema at night, and we twins held tight to Bee's hands. It was like entering a palace, and the curtains across the screen, rippling with magical, ever-changing colours, were the most beautiful things we had ever seen. To make our happiness complete – or it would have been if we hadn't been worried about Father and Mother missing the treat – the film was *On Moonlight Bay* starring Doris Day. We staggered out, drunk with pleasure, into the middle of the night. But there was more; Bee bought us chips on the way home. Drizzle was making haloes around the street lights, we had seen Doris Day, and our choice of favourite film star and our collection of cigarette cards was vindicated; we were real people, with lips and fingers stinging with salt and vinegar.

'What the bloody hell time of night do you call this?'

Father was waiting in the hall, wearing a sleeveless pullover and pyjama trousers, waving an alarm clock.

The house seemed dark when we got home from school the next day. It was cold. Mother was kneeling in front of the fire trying to blaze up the wet coal with a newspaper. She had cut her finger on the bread knife and a thick drop of blood splashed on to the tiled fireplace. Bee had gone.

Suzannah and Maria are still with us, as reminders of Auntie Bee. In a manner of speaking. You see, their heads and limbs were attached to their bodies with elastic bands and over the years they had many adventures, until somehow there were just enough parts to make up one doll. We call her Zan-Mri now. It does seem a shame that Auntie Bee, who gave her to us, never married. She was wonderful with children.

As she leaves the office Catriona Ling swallows two Quiet Life tablets and drops her paper cup into a wastebin full of crumpled paper and cigarette butts. She is feeling sick with the apprehension that curdles her life like sour milk. Bee, she remembers, used to smoke some exotic brand, De Reszke or Du Maurier or Black Cat, screwing a cigarette into a green and black holder banded in marcasite with her red-tipped nails, flicking her lighter at Mother's Woodbine. Catriona wishes that she had not lost the deco cigarette case that somebody once gave her because it is important that she appears to be a success. She is afraid that she will regress to a four year old, blurting out her troubles to Bee. She is regretting her impulse to telephone her, and is worried about her choice of restaurant, which, convenient for her, will mean that Bee will probably have to take a taxi. Anxiety buzzes away, under the grief of a recent bereavement; there is her old uncle, her father's only surviving brother for whom Catriona has somehow become responsible; the women's publishing co-operative in which she is a partner is in dire financial straits; there are friends in hospital she should be visiting, calls she is too tired and dispirited to return when she gets home in the evenings, the heating in her flat is on the blink, ready to fail at the first really cold weather, the Hoover is broken, the mortgage huge, the car due for a service, her cat is on tablets, hence the scratches on her hands, and her lover, Rachel, has volunteered to take part in a late-night television programme where unattractive people talk frankly about their sexual practices. And she had meant to have her hair cut before seeing Bee.

A wind whips her across Covent Garden, and the sight of people bedded down in doorways does not make her count her blessings; instead the dark shapes are absorbed into her despair. At least she has arrived before Bee, but her relief is swamped by terror that she has got the wrong place, the wrong time. Noise bounces off the tiled walls as she sips a glass of wine and she knows that she should have chosen somewhere more *intime*. But for what? To tell Bee that she was sorry that they hadn't invited her to Mother's funeral? To say that she, Catriona, had never forgotten her first sight of Bee swinging along the road, of her turbaned head and houndstooth jacket flaring from padded shoulders, her red lipsticked mouth, and wide black trousers skimming thickly high-heeled black suede shoes? To mumble how Bee's risky glamour set her above the respectable neighbours and teachers with their hair in buns like dried figs, and that she had always had a thing about trouser ladies? Or to confess how, later, any old collar-and-tie job hunched over a pint of Guinness would set her young heart racing as if one of those pinstriped pockets held the key to the world she was desperate to enter, and how, in her teens, she had lurked outside clubs, not daring to ask anybody to take her in? Should she risk confiding that only she, of all the family, could guess what hell that visit to Canterbury had been for Bee? Then she sees Bee, walking a bit stiffly, leaning on a silver-topped cane, being led by a waiter towards her table.

Bee, treading carefully so as not to slip on the floor, which feels like an ice rink as pain flares around her hip joints, has a sudden memory of Alec slamming down his miner's helmet with its lamp on the kitchen table, and his snap tin and dudley – metal lunch box and water bottle – in hard, shiny, male challenge to her, and sees his eyes glaring out of the grimy face, which he has left unwashed, and the blue coal-dust scars under the skin of his arms. And Betty is standing up and waving to her across the restaurant, the light catching the crinkle-crankle, zig-zag, rick-rack hair; except that it is Catriona, of course, who is kissing her awkwardly on both cheeks now, bumping her nose.

Bee hadn't meant to say it so soon, but putting down her glass, while they are waiting for the starters, she hears herself, 'I was rather puzzled – and very upset to tell the truth – to get a birthday card from the twins. Signed by them both. When, you know, you told me the dreadful news on the telephone – that Erica has died. I didn't know what to think. I'm sorry, I didn't mean to upset you, my dear ...'

'No, it's all right. I mean, it isn't really at all. But you haven't upset me. It's difficult to explain. We're all upset, Donald and Jamie and their families, but you remember how the twins were always a bit – odd. Different. They never – I mean, I don't suppose you recall those dolls you gave them, Suzannah and Maria – well, anyway, over the years they, Heather and Erica, sort of – amalgamated. As far as Erica's, I mean, Heather's concerned, they're both still there, nothing has changed. So we go along with it ...'

Catriona is looking helplessly at Bee when the food arrives.

Neither of them wants it.

'Are the twins still crazy about Doris Day?' Bee asks resolutely, dipping a bit of bread into olive oil.

'Oh yes!'

In fact, Catriona and Rachel have a tape of Doris Day's greatest hits, which they like to play full blast in the car. She doesn't tell Bee how Father took them all to see *By the Light of the Silvery Moon*, the sequel to *On Moonlight Bay*, a couple of years after Bee's flight from Canterbury, or how she and Mother had wept, each for her own reasons, while watching *Calamity Jane* on television not long before Mother died, or say that the scene where Calamity and Adelaide Adams transform Calam's filthy cabin into a pretty love-nest for two always breaks her heart. 'A woman and a whisk broom can accomplish oh so much, so never underestimate a woman's touch!' The film should have ended there, with the two of them so obviously in love. 'With the magic of a broom she can mesmerise a room.' Catriona resolves to try to put the romance back in her marriage when she gets home tonight by the light of the silvery moon. Then, aware that a long silence is hanging over their table in the clamour all around them, she looks up.

Bee, the birthday girl, is raising her glass in salute, smiling across glistening strips of red and yellow peppers on painted plates, saying, 'This is fun!', and Catriona sees that Bee, the good old trouper, is going to make the evening all right.

The Index of Embarrassment

We were in my uncle's study, Bob, his dog Fido and I, when he started telling me about a visit from his next-door neighbour Martha earlier that morning. Uncle Bob sprawled in his chair like a slack-bodied snake digesting some live prey, his eyes flickering off the Harvey Nicks carrier bag in my hand.

'Martha said, with uncharacteristic delicacy, "We noticed the – odour."'

'She said *what?*'

Uncle Bob believes that soap and water destroy the skin's essential oils. His plump pink cheeks, the long beard which he sometimes wears in a plait and the white ponytail sticking out of his baseball cap have a tallowy gleam, and as he considers household chores to be women's work and there wasn't one around, things had got a bit out of hand. Was it Bob's drains, his dustbin, his dog, his socks or his person which had provoked this insult? I was surprised by a rush of family loyalty, but luckily, before I could put my foot in it, he went on, 'He must have been in the bath for a while, if he was – stinking.'

Bob masticated the word. Everything has to be oblique with him; his pronouncements can be difficult to decipher. His masterwork, *The Definitive Index of Embarrassment*, was ranged in files on the shelves of the study, which was the front room of his ground-floor flat. Newspapers and magazines were stacked on the floor. I had always been a bit scared of him, and it was only now that I was no spring chicken myself that I felt grown-up enough to dare to say,

'I don't understand. Who was in his bath, and why did he stink? Surely whoever it was would be very clean if he'd been there a long time?'

Uncle Bob's lips tightened, working themselves up to express a conventional sentiment. Martha is a pillar or something smaller, such as a hassock, of a local evangelical church; she's tiny, knee-high to a grasshopper, like me. Her porch is usually crammed with cash-and-carry cases of soft drinks for post-service refreshments, and it was her piety which made me think of Lazarus in the Bible – 'by this time he stinketh'. But presumably this guy, whoever he was, had simply been accused of shower-gel pollution or bath-essence abuse, or so I hoped. I imagined Martha wrinkling her nose at a drifting cluster of malodorous pink bubbles. Nobody but Bob could have charged her with indelicacy.

'I'm sorry to report, nephew o' mine,' Uncle Bob said, 'that we have lost Neighbour Dennis. The police had to break in to take him away.'

'Why?'

Dennis lived in the upstairs flat of the house on the other side of Martha's. I only knew him to say hello.

Then the blood rushed from my head and I sat down, picturing Dennis white and bloated, decomposing in a bathtub of red water.

'Martha said, and she didn't make any other comment, that it was never women who came to call. Friend Dennis's visitors were all men. The implication, I very much regret, seemed to be that our Mr Jennings was a bit of a lowlife.'

Fido settled on my feet like a mildewed chenille bathmat.

'Do the police think it was suicide then – or murder?'

I was uncomfortable, a voyeur spying through the keyhole at Dennis naked in his bath, and I felt like a ghoul presuming on my slight acquaintance with him in suggesting that Dennis might have been killed. Yet as I uttered the word 'Murder', which the television news and drama has robbed of its power to shock, it took on its true shape and hung ghastly and terrifying in that quiet room with a dog snoring in a pool of February sunshine.

'Could it have been – natural causes?' I asked then, in the faint hope that a congenital weakness might make the death of a man in his forties somehow, well, less – unnatural, even though I had known lots of people younger than Dennis who'd gone. Bob shook his head.

'Didn't he have a mother? When he borrowed your stepladder, wasn't he fixing the place up for her to come to stay?'

'One might be forgiven for trusting a chap to have the

107

decency to put his affairs in order if he intended to do away with himself, don't you think, Freddy? I let him take that ladder, against my better judgement, a good six weeks ago and I haven't heard a peep out of him since. Nor will again, I suppose. In fact, the more consideration I give to his story, the less I am inclined to believe that he had a mother at all. However, should such a person exist, no doubt she is ensconced in Number fifteen now, clawing through the deceased's effects and making such arrangements as are required for the disposal of a body in unhallowed ground.'

'Fair dos, Uncle Bob,' I bleated, despising myself for not walking out on the old bastard. My sister Iris would have been halfway down the street by now.

I had probably attended more funerals than Uncle Bob had had hot dinners; his Meals on Wheels foil dishes were on the floor. Sometimes I ate the puddings, but today Fido had got there first. It seemed so sad that a mother should have had a little baby way back in the Fifties, and named him Dennis, only for it all to end like this. She must have written his name in biro in his wellies, Dennis Jennings, and hung his gloves on elastic through his coat sleeves, and called him Dennis the Menace when he was naughty. I could see that Bob was more concerned with the loss of his ladder than of his neighbour, so I said that I'd better be going to the shops, before he could send me round to the house of horror to reclaim it, offering my condolences to a grieving mother as I clattered out with the aluminium legs high-kicking under my arm.

I took the shopping bag and list and set off, with Fido waddling in front of me. The wind lifted his ears and rippled his coat, so that for a moment he looked quite lively, and I wondered briefly what was the point of him and whether he had any race-memory of running in a pack with his wild ancestors, and I felt a stab of pity for his debased existence. It was a long time since this splay-footed eater of processed food had felt grass beneath his pads, or any surface but the pavement between Colley Gardens and Albion Minimart. Uncle Bob had named him Fido as a sort of joke, for of course the poor mutt had no option; cats can clear off if they like, but infidelity isn't in a dog's nature. There used to be loads of dogs here, pit bulls and Rottweilers and Dobermanns, bandy-legged scarred dogs used for fighting, but the government stuck them all on death row, family pets, convicted maulers and drug dealers' bodyguards alike, and now you see hardly any except the long-haired Alsatians in the shops. Fido and I had to pass Dennis's house. I averted my eyes, and he lifted his leg over the gatepost.

Uncle Bob is virtually a recluse now; age and his natural misanthropy making it difficult for him to leave the house. I don't mind doing his shopping because other people's shops are always more interesting than one's own, and I am a hotel night porter, and don't sleep much during the day. In fact, I usually manage to snatch a catnap or two at the desk, despite the video camera trained on the lobby. Vincents Hotel, off Chelsea Green, advertises itself as one of London's best-kept secrets; it's chintzy, discreet and over-priced, and I fit in there very well.

When I was a boy, I assumed that I would grow up into the sort of person who listens to Radio Three and goes to concerts at the Wigmore Hall or St John's, Smith Square, yet here I am, my mind permanently tuned to Capital Gold and Country 10.35 AM, the opera buff inside me still trying to get out. Although Bob despises me as a physical and intellectual lightweight, I'm the only one of the family with whom he hasn't quarrelled, and I'm useful in that I've been able to help him out with many an embarrassing line from a song which should never have been allowed within a mile of a recording studio. It's my proud boast that I never forget a phrase.

Only last week, I'd provided Bob with a couple of corkers for the food section of his Embarrassing Lyrics file – the oldies but goodies, 'Frankfurter Sandwiches' and 'Pineapple Princess', and he has me to thank for 'Johnny Get Angry' and 'Friendly Persuasion' ('Thee pleasures me in a thousand ways') of the same era, and many a golden turkey plucked from the pages of Sir Cliff's songbook. My personal *bête noire* is the phrase 'keep me satisfied'; it really makes my skin crawl, conjuring up an exhausted sex-slave in thrall to lusts which have nothing to do with love. Be that as it may, Bob's tragedy is that despite having lived through the Radio Luxemburg years and being the Casaubon of Colley Gardens, he has a tin ear, a poor memory and lacks the fundamental ability to differentiate between the poignant and the embarrassing. 'I heard a good one on the wireless today, Freddy,' he told me once, '"Nobody Loves a Fairy When She's Forty."' 'That's not embarrassing, it's sad,' I said. 'Anyway, Mum's still got our old fairy dolly; Christmas wouldn't be Christmas without fairy dolly perched on top of the tree.' And I'd had to delete Dolly Parton's 'The Bargain Store' from the shopping when I was inserting 'Rabbit, Rabbit, Rabbit' by those chirpy cockney sparrows (ain't it a shame sparrers can't sing?) Chas and Dave. That's rabbit as in rabbit and pork – talk, and this geezer's bird's 'got more rabbit than Sainsbury's', whereas in all my wide retail experience I've never encountered a single member of the family Leporidae, unless you admit the petfood display, which actually I don't, in any of Mr Sainsbury's establishments.

Perhaps fortunately, the Internet had come too late for Uncle Bob; true, he was at risk from drowning in newsprint, but access to the Web would have driven him right over the edge, like a mad spider. Nevertheless, it was kind of melancholy to visualize his magnum opus heaped in a skip outside Number Eleven, or in the black sacks of the vultures who clear the houses of the dead. The worst-case scenario, though, would be that he left the lot to me. It might seem strange that Bob, who has on more than one occasion been spotted in Albion Road in his pyjamas, and secures his beard with a rubber band or a twist of plastic wire, should have set himself up as an authority on embarrassment, but there it is. He was a fighter pilot in the war, risking his life to make the world a safe place for wimps like me, and thereafter a civil servant, so I guess he is entitled to spend his retirement as he wishes.

The *Index* started out as a hobby, a scrapbook of humorous and humiliating stories gleaned from the media, became a sort of thesis entitled *Seven Types of Embarrassment*, and then like Topsy (see under *Clichés*), it just growed. Into an obsession. The man's a fool, though; he's got *Magnificent Obsession* listed in the Hollywood file, whereas I'm a total Douglas Sirk freak. As for personal embarrassment, my sister and I ingested it with our mother's milk (Cow & Gate naturally). Iris was twenty-five before she could walk across a room. But she beat it and now she's a gynaecologist, married with two great kids. Anyway, as I've come to realize, embarrassmentology is an inexact science, it's all relative — and uncles can be the most embarrassing relatives of all.

Minimart was doing a nice line in square silver scourers, so I bought a couple, as well as Bob's groceries and the local paper. Bob had checked out the nationals, but I thought there might be something about Dennis there. I did feel slightly ashamed, even if it was the best way of finding out without engaging in gossip with the shop people or Martha. A depressed-looking woman was choosing five valentines, probably for her daughters; that would have tickled Uncle Bob, but I wasn't going to share it with him. Walking back along Colley Gardens, and the address is something of a misnomer now, Fido got tangled up in loops of the cassette tape that always seems to be blowing about. Again I avoided looking at Dennis's house; I didn't want to know what was going on inside, or to imagine his state of mind as he died. A rook was going 'carp carp carp' on a chimney across the street and I noticed the tips of bulbs pushing up through a crushed polystyrene cup beside Bob's dustbin.

'Here it is,' I said to Bob, opening the paper, 'MAN FOUND DEAD.'

'Hold the front page. That should sell a lot of copies round here. *Man Found Alive*, now that would be a story.'

'It's the wrong bloke,' I said, reading on about a pensioner discovered in a maggotty condition. 'It's not him.'

'Just another sad little south London death,' said Bob, adding, 'it is not *he*.'

I crumpled the newspaper into the bin, not wanting Bob

to read it. It struck me that people in our family, after lives filled with love affairs and adventure and admirers, have an unfortunate habit of ending up alone in rented rooms. At least I owned my place, be it never so humble, but there was somebody else living there with me whom I had begun to neglect. It's awful, isn't it, how that happens; as if you bid for a beautiful plate in an auction, and then after a few months, you risk bunging it the dishwasher, telling yourself it won't hurt just the once, and before you know it, it becomes a habit and your plate's chipped and the pattern faded. A lurking fear, unformed until now, that I would turn into Uncle Bob, settled heavily on me, and I decided to stop off at M&S for an American-style cheesecake that Jacob liked – I'd been nagging him about his weight recently – and pick up some flowers at the tube station.

Bob had his finger in the pot of Gentleman's Relish I'd brought. It turned my stomach to look at him.

'I forgot to give you a gobbet of embarrassing information,' I said, 'a mere titbit, a *bonne bouche*, an *amuse gueule* …'

'Spit it out,' said Bob.

'On my way here I noticed that the name of the Duke of Clarence pub has been changed to the Ant and Artichoke.'

Bob, a self-appointed recording angel with a red biro, noted down grimly this latest example of human folly.

'What a cheap trick,' he said.

'Who is?' I quipped.

'What kind of a scoundrel would invent a mother to get his hands on an elderly and not at all robust chap's stepladder?'

'You tell me,' I said. 'Well, Bob, I suppose I'd better be making tracks.'

Panic flashed in his eyes as he said, 'Like a snail. Couldn't you manage another cuppa? Perhaps you'd like to wash your hands? You've got a long journey.'

'I'm fine thanks.'

Uncle Bob always managed to imply that he had no use for a lavatory himself, but kept one purely for the convenience of incontinent visitors such as myself.

'Well, I mustn't keep you from your work.'

He plaited his beard nervously, dismissing my job with a bitter smile that suggested some house of ill-repute. He never asked me about my life, either from lack of interest or because he didn't want to know, but as his misogyny equalled his homophobia it suited me not to subject any of my friends to his scorn even at a distance. Take Lady Brenda, for example. He would have had a field day with her.

Lady Brenda is a permanent resident at Vincents and has lived in a suite of two rooms on the fourth floor since the year dot. I have to fetch her fur coat, chilled and smelling of mothballs, from the fridge when she goes out in the evenings and help her into it. She's ninety if she's a day, and her legs are heavily bandaged and she walks with two sticks. She looks a right old *roué*, rouged and decked with paste jewellery, but I have a lot of time for her. You don't find many nonagenarians making the effort to go down the pub every night, and as I often tell Jacob, she is an example to us all. She only has a couple of Guinesses, but she's well away when she gets back, and we have some brilliant conversations, and she's given me some of her late husband's cufflinks. I only hope I'm half as good as she is when I'm her age.

'We're two of a kind, Freddy,' she said once.

After I'd put her in the lift, I studied myself in the mirror above the desk, and I saw what I might become; one of those bad-tempered elderly elves working behind a bar, with a cinched-in waist and tiny bum and the lined face of a disgraced jockey. Actually, I did start out in the racing game, after I was invited to leave school, as a stable lad at Lamberhurst, but I fell from grace on my first day. Grace was a mean donkey, the travelling companion of a nervous gelding, and she ended my career on the turf.

My father was a second violinist. He was run over by a taxi while nipping out for an interval drink, and it was a struggle for my mother to provide for us. We were always keeping up appearances. She was a needlework teacher, and she felt the shame of my father's demise deeply. I don't recall her brother, Uncle Bob, being around much to help. He usually had some woman in tow, some poor sap who thought she would be the one to tame him; for a man who despised women he certainly had a lot of mistresses, but that's often the way. The last one, Audrey, who knitted him socks, had thrown in the tea-towel a month ago; perhaps she had found her file. Bob's pet name for her was Tawdry. I was pretty sure he had a file on me too, stashed behind *The Greengrocer's Apostrophe* and *The Human Body*.

'Have you noticed, Freddy,' he asked me once, 'the ugliness of anatomical terminology? Perhaps justifiably so. Tastebuds,' he enunciated, 'gland. Membrane. Tonsils. Toenails. Scrotum.' His mouth was moist with distaste.

So why did I go on visiting him? I think it was because I felt sorry for him, although Iris said he was just using me and Jacob insisted it was a symbiotic relationship of parasite and host, though I wouldn't know who was which.

'See you next week, then,' I said, and a wave of dreariness swept over me as I reflected how my pleasure in snouting out snippets for the *Index* had long since palled. The truth was, the older I got, the less embarrassing I found everything; life, people, words. I mean, I can exchange a quip with the best of them now and employ expressions like 'the year dot' without turning a hair or batting a proverbial.

Martha was going into her house as I came out of Bob's.
'How did you find Uncle today?' she asked.

'Oh, not too bad, thanks, Martha. But not too good, either, if you know what I mean.'

'I know what you mean! We're none of us *too* good, eh? But we try, we keep on trying.'

She was laughing as she shut her door. And then I saw a woman standing in the front garden of Dennis's house.

My instinct was to cross the road, but I made myself walk towards her.

'Mrs Jennings?'

She was smartly dressed in chain-store pastels, with pale blue eyeshadow on swollen lids and coral lipstick and a perky daffodil yellow scarf. She looked as if she had her hair done for the occasion of identifying her son's body. Dennis's mother was a type of woman for whom I have a lot of respect; the sort who works in a shoe shop all her life and makes the best of herself, smiling at the customer when her own feet are killing her.

'I just want to say how sorry I am.'

'Thank you.'

'If there's anything I can do …'

'Not really, I don't suppose. But thanks anyway. Did you know – my son?'

'Not well. We met once or twice, in passing. But my uncle, at Number Eleven, knew Dennis and he always spoke very highly of him.'

'So Bob's your uncle?'

That's how somebody caught up in a hideous tragedy

smiles, I thought, that's the crooked way the mouth goes.

'Fraid so.'

'I believe there's a ladder belongs to him, indoors. I'll fetch it round later.'

'No, don't. You mustn't. I'll take it.'

It was imperative to keep this woman as far away from Uncle Bob as possible. She must not set foot over his threshold. His sharp nose would sniff out the loneliness masked by her rather shrill perfume and he would home in on the vulnerable heart beneath the peachskin mac, biding his time before going for the jugular hidden by that brave yellow scarf.

'It's no trouble,' she said.

'No, really, I insist. I'll do it now.'

'I wasn't going to run off with it, you know. I'm sure Dennis would have returned it himself, if –'

'Oh God – I didn't mean – I'm so sorry, so sorry.'

'Don't,' she said. 'You'll start me off again. Here.'

She opened her handbag and gave me a mauve tissue.

'This is so embarrassing. It's all the wrong way round –'

I wiped my eyes.

'I'd offer you a cup of tea,' she said, 'only …'

I thought she meant that I might be squeamish about going into the flat.

'That would be great. I could murder a cup of tea!'

'Only, there isn't any, I was going to say. Not one single solitary teabag.'

A Silver Summer

In the summer of 1962, a girl sits at the edge of the lunchtime pastoral in Lincoln's Inn Fields. Although she is alone among the flowers and bees mumbling in old, sun-warmed stone, she is not a wallflower herself, merely waiting to be asked to join the dance. Meanwhile she observes the quadrangle quadrilles, the furtive two-steps, a fandango of fantails in the blue air above white discarded shirts and white legs in rolled-down stockings. Barristers stroll across the daisied grass, swinging the big blue bags that contain their official robes, and if any whiff of corruption escapes those tasselled drawstrings, Tessa, daydreaming in the scent of roses, cannot smell it and is reminded of shoebags on the pegs at the school she left three months ago, and thinks how far away it seems. Her glossy hair, cut in a fringe above green eyes, is iridescent like starlings' feathers in the sun. She has just made an appointment at a Hebe Hair Salon, which will rather spoil it.

Her lunch hour over, Tessa returns to Sheldon's Silver & Antiques in Chancery Lane. Mrs Sheldon has an aura of Chanel and Lalique, *poudre de riz* and Biarritz. She flies to the Riviera every January with her sister and has photographs of the two of them on the Promenade Des Anglais at Nice, with a famous bandleader of the Thirties. Mrs Sheldon smokes Black Cat in an amber cigarette holder, and her cough, like her rage, is formidable. Tessa worships her and thinks she has a heart of gold. Well, silver-gilt, perhaps. Pinchbeck anyway. Tessa is learning fast; she studies the little book of silver hallmarks on the train on her way home each evening.

'I've been rushed off my feet, Tessa!' Mrs Sheldon accuses. 'Get me a cup of tea, there's a good girl, and then we'll need some boxes from over the road.'

The first order is fine, because Tessa likes going to the Italian café next door and saying, 'Tea for the Lady, please,' as she's been instructed, so that Alf will make it precisely to Mrs Sheldon's requirements. The café is always steamy, busy and noisy, with Ilda, Alf's sister, shouting, 'Chump chop and chips twice, right away!' to the cook.

The second command fills her with dread. Going across to Dodd and Dodsworth's, the Legal Stationers, to ask for spare boxes is the only aspect of her job which she hates.

'The boy will take you down to the cellar for a look,' says courteous, obliging, old Mr Dodsworth.

'For a feel, don't you mean?' mouths the Dodd and Dodsworth boy, through wet, slack lips, and then says loudly, 'Follow me, Modom, *if* you please!'

Paunchy at nineteen, in a shiny blue suit, with a complexion suggestive of solitary pleasures, the Dodd and

Dodsworth boy leads the way. As soon as they are in the cellar, he switches off the light and pushes her against a stack of stationery. Today, Tessa escapes with a grazed lip and faint bruises on the arms that clutch a pair of cardboard boxes.

'Don't lounge there with your hands in your pockets, boy. Smarten yourself up,' Tessa hears old Mr Dodsworth say as he holds open the door for her.

'Yes, sir,' says the Dodd and Dodsworth boy.

Mrs Sheldon is fuming, about to lose a sale.

Business is good. The tourists, Swedish and American, are buying silver; Nigerian law students in bright patterned cotton robes and headdresses are buying gold; freemasons are buying seals and fobs and gold balls that open to reveal secret symbols for their watch chains; nurses are buying filigree silver belt-buckles; judges are buying Spy cartoons to hang in their Chambers. Mrs Sheldon's great-niece Natalie comes in to help sometimes, freeing Tessa to take and collect repairs from the bead-stringers in Hatton Garden and the engravers and silversmiths in Clerkenwell. She loves walking through Leather Lane market and climbing dark, splintery staircases in ancient buildings, trusted with precious things. And yet sometimes, in the hot, glittery streets and the gardens of Lincoln's Inn, she feels a little lonely.

A dealer, one of those mysterious men who pull

diamonds and bits of jewellery in twists of tissue paper from hidden pockets, asks her for a date. He is at least forty and Tessa is glad when Mrs Sheldon refuses on her behalf. A young barrister takes her to lunch at a Chinese restaurant, where the waiter scorns her for being vegetarian, and a clerk begins to wait for her at the top of the escalator each morning. Mrs Sheldon is so pleased with Tessa's work that she gives her an old paste ring with a stone like a cabochon ruby. Tessa buys her mother a little gold brooch with MIZPAH on it.

'Wasn't there one that said "Daphne"?' her mother asks, but she wears the brooch every day, round the house. She tells Tessa not to worry, the right boy will come along some day.

It is a sultry afternoon, just before closing time, when a woman buys the Capodimonte figures of the Four Seasons. Tessa is told to run across the road for a stout box.

'Please be quick, I'm in a hurry!' she pleads with the Dodd and Dodsworth boy, staying safely halfway down the cellar stairs.

'I'll bet you are!'

He drags her off the step into darkness as he flicks off the light, crushing her against him, pressing her closed fist on his swollen trousers, as they struggle, trying to get his hand up her skirt.

'Begging for it, aren't you?' he pants. 'I've been watching you! I bet you've had it off with half the blokes down Leather Lane.'

Tessa wrenches a hand free and hits him hard across the face. She gropes for the light switch and grabs a box. As she backs up the stairs, fearful of a hand shooting out to grasp her ankle, she sees, horrified, a pigeon's egg ruby of blood welling from the corner of his lip, where her ring had caught it.

'Shouldn't have done that,' he says. A fat tongue flips the ruby into his mouth.

Cars brake and hoot as Tessa runs through the traffic, and trips over the kerb.

'Hey, are you OK?'

She sees a blur of olive skin, blond curls, blue denim, and feels a hand on her arm, helping her up.

'Yes, yes, I'm fine, thanks.'

She rushes inside. Her face is on fire, and her hands feel filthy as she swaddles the porcelain babies in newspaper and tissue and tucks them into a bed of wood-wool. Too humiliated to speak of the incident ever, to anybody, she plans desperate stratagems for getting out of going to Dodd and Dodsworth's again, and scrubs her hands sore at the sink, dragging the cabochon ruby from her finger.

She is on her way to the tube, passing the Silver Vaults,

when a boy falls into step beside her, making her jump. He pulls her back from the gutter on to the pavement.

'Is this your day for getting run over? I'm sorry – I didn't mean to startle you. I was hoping you'd come this way. Just tell me to get lost if I'm bothering you. I'm Tyler,' he adds hopefully.

Tessa realizes that she is with the most beautiful boy she has ever seen.

'No, it's all right. I was just on my way home. I'm Tessa.'

'Well, Tessa, could I buy you a cup of coffee or something?' A shiny blue suit pushes past them, unnoticed.

'You're American, aren't you?' says Tessa as they walk on.

'From New York. On vacation. I'm just here in London for another few days before joining up with friends in Paris. Doesn't seem like such a hot idea now.'

'What doesn't?'

'Paris. Now that I've met you.'

Tessa phones her mother to say she will be late. They walk, and talk, until they come upon a little restaurant called San Marino. Although it is still early, the waiter sets a candle in a chianti bottle on their table, and sings 'O Sole Mio' as he waltzes around with the cutlery, under the plastic vine leaves hung with coloured fairylights. They can't get over how much they have in common, music, films, books, and the most amazing thing is, apart from the fact they might never have met, that Tyler's mother used to sell jewellery in Bloomingdale's. Later, on the Embankment, they kiss under a green sky with faint hazy stars, while the tide tries to race away with the reflections of the shimmering glass globes that loop the river.

Alf is in a bad mood the next morning when Tessa goes in for Mrs Sheldon's tea and a cup for herself.

'That's the one for the *Lady* ...', he says, as if she didn't know by now.

And Ilda is moaning about the veal or salami or something.

'Easy meat!' she mutters fiercely.

Tessa is too excited to pay them much attention. Tyler is meeting her for lunch.

Mrs Sheldon is in a foul temper too. Perhaps it's the weather; the sky is oppressive with heavy clouds like Old Sheffield plate with the copper wearing through. Business is slow. Mrs Sheldon abruptly tells Tessa to get on with cleaning some silver. She strides up and down the shop with a long ash on her cigarette. Silver shivers on the glass shelves at every sharp turn of her high heels, porcelain tinkles in fear. You could cut the air with the verdigrised knife Tessa is dunking into the malodorous Silver Dip. A fine powder drifts over her hair and dress, into her nose, as she brushes polish from grooves and interstices. By mid-morning her hands are grey. She sits like Cinderella, wondering what she has done wrong, while Mrs Sheldon serves the customers.

At a quarter to one, she glances out of the window.

Shock sucks the breath and colour from her as if with a straw, and blows it back again, flooding her face with icy red. Tyler is across the street, talking to the Dodd and Dodsworth boy.

'Nn-oh!' Tessa screams, jumping up, upsetting the Silver Dip, tangling with a long-coated *schnorrer* in the doorway, deaf to his curse. Tyler starts running.

'Tyler! Wait! Oh, please wait. Tyler!'

She chases him to the tube, glimpsing his blond head, his long blue legs through gaps in the crowded pavement. She almost has him, and grasps air with her grey hands. Then she knows she has lost him.

Ilda's words 'Easy meat' slap her face, like a raw, dirty slice of veal, as she understands their meaning. The fat worm of lust and malice that lurks in those blue trousers has impelled the Dodd and Dodsworth boy up and down the Lane to do its spiteful work. She turns back towards the shop, where everything is tarnished now. The loss of Tyler and the disgrace are too much to bear. She finds herself in Lincoln's Inn Fields, sobbing into the grass.

Eventually she sits up, wiping the falling tears with the backs of her hands, leaving great smears. 'I *will* find him again, whatever it takes. I'll go to, to Bloomingdale's, to the

Ivy League, whatever that is, they'll be able to help me trace him and tell him the truth.'

Tessa walks back slowly, as the sky, like a battered old salver, starts oozing drops of Silver Dip. People would say, 'There's no smoke without fire.' Throw a bit of mud, and some of it sticks, she knows. Well, sticks and stones might break her bones, but names would never hurt her! She is a drowned grey rat, but determined, by the time she reaches the shop; full of plans for making smoke and fire in a certain cellar, for which somebody else would be blamed, and for throwing mud and making it stick.

The Day of the Gecko

When the official part of the trip, at the World Book Fair in Delhi, was over, Alicia and her assistant Natasha flew to Goa. The road from the airport wound downward to the sea through banyans, trailing creepers and banana trees, passing grazing cattle and marshes of small white water lilies standing erect on their stems. The taxi hit a bump and in her mind's eye Allie saw her suitcase flying from the boot, spilling books and business clothes, and submerging with a splash and scattering of storks. She wondered if she would care if it did happen. After the heat and hassle of the city, the angst of travelling and hotel life, she could see how a person might be seduced by the surrounding lushness and enervated by the green humidity.

Now and then they glimpsed houses with verandas and wooden balconies breasting the foliage, pot-bellied pigs, black with pink stockings, rooting in the dust, goats and chickens, buffaloes. As each house was swallowed up behind them, Allie thought, her heartbeat quickening, perhaps that's the one. Maybe that's where Eric Alabaster has gone to ground. And, with a pang, she wondered if that woman carrying a bundle of reeds on her head might be Eric's wife or if any of the schoolchildren in their bright blue uniforms and flip-flops could be his.

Eric Alabaster had published four novels between 1970 and 1985 and then he had disappeared. He had always been a reclusive yet charismatic figure, a sun-bleached traveller, and when it became apparent that he had gone missing several men claimed to have been his closest friend and various women declared that he had been in love with them. Alabaster had no family, except some cousins in Australia with whom he hadn't kept in touch. For a while it became common knowledge that Alabaster was an international arms dealer, a spy, a double agent working both for and against the government. Rumours of murder or suicide and speculation as to his whereabouts died down as the years passed, although his name still bobbed up like a cork from time to time in conversation and literary criticism. It was not until one of her authors had come forward with the idea of writing his biography that Allie read Alabaster's books and determined to relaunch them to coincide with the publication of the *Life*. Alicia Compton was the editorial director of a small publishing house which had been taken over by a large conglomerate and for the time being at least it seemed that she had a free hand to develop her list. With apparent casualness she made enquiries among Eric Alabaster's former associates which led her nowhere, and as far as his former publisher was concerned, the trail had gone cold in India.

It had seemed to Allie as she read the novels that Alabaster was speaking directly to her; she was his first reader, the one for whom the books had been written. They were exactly the same age. She had gazed at the pictures on his bookjackets until his lips almost moved in a smile, and then, as she planned her trip to Delhi, it was as if a bottle had been washed ashore at her feet. A bottle tossed into the Arabian Sea containing the message that Eric Alabaster was waiting for her in Goa. It was the perfect place to disappear, and who knew what masterwork might have been penned beside that turquoise sea? With his white-blond hair and light eyes he should not be hard to identify.

Allie became aware of Tasha's conversation with the taxi driver.

'Why are you coming here?' he was asking. 'You should go to north Goa where more tourists are going.'

'That's why we came here. We don't want to be tourists. Actually, we're sort of looking for somebody.'

'I think you're looking for me.'

'Take it easy, Tasha,' muttered Allie, regretting not for the first time that Tasha would be her companion in this earthly paradise; Tasha in India had proved quite a different person from the London Tasha, or perhaps, having cast off her metropolitan black, she was showing herself in her true colours. Allie's briefcase was full of the cards of publishers and academics, unsolicited manuscripts and those of the two writers she had signed up, while Tasha's wallet bulged with the scribbled names and addresses of boys in carpet shops and hotel waiters, the cards of jewellers and the man from whom she'd bought her Pashmina shawl. It would serve Tasha right if that mahout she had got so friendly with in Delhi turned up on her doorstep in Fulham with his elephant. Tasha Calloway was generally described as gamine; to Allie, her face was like a cat's, who rubs against your legs while knowing there is a dead bird behind the sofa.

Tasha had let her down badly in Delhi, taking off on a day's jaunt to the Taj Mahal, leaving Allie to cope alone with a portfolio of appointments. She had tossed Allie one of her postcards of the Taj, saying, 'You can send it to somebody and pretend you saw it yourself. After all, everybody knows what it looks like.' Now, through the taxi window, Allie could see coconut palms soaring against the hot blue sky. 'There will be plenty more pebbles on the beach,' she told Tasha, 'or fish in the sea.'

'Will you answer me something?' the driver asked. 'Why it is you people like to be naked on the beach?'

Before Tasha could reply, Allie said, 'No, you answer me something. How far is it to the Da Silva Guest House?'

'We are there, mamma.'

The Da Silva Guest House was composed of the original structure, where the family lived, and five built-on apartments which faced the sea. A shrine to the Virgin was set into the front wall of the house, and roses, hibiscus and jacaranda wreathed the veranda and wooden shutters. Each apartment was designed to take two people but although Allie, enchanted by the guest house's careless perfection, said that she was willing to share, she was relieved when Tasha insisted it would be better if they each had their own space. Allie was shown to Number Three, Tasha to Number Five. They saw a young couple disappearing into Number Four. 'Honeymooners,' Tasha mouthed, under the noise of the crows who strutted and flapped in the palm trees, cawing ceaselessly. As soon as they had dealt with the formalities, the women put on their swimming costumes under their clothes, slathered themselves in mosquito repellent and as low-protection sun cream as they dared, and headed for the beach.

'Mad dogs and Englishwomen', observed Tasha, as they walked the short distance.

They had seen several dogs already, pretty dogs with pricked ears, quite unlike the sad, scabby creatures that slunk about the city. Notices in their rooms had warned against wandering on deserted parts of the beach after sunset, particularly if they were scantily dressed, unless they were able to defend themselves.

'I've got a gecko in my cupboard,' said Tasha.

A gecko? It was a sign. *The Gecko* was Allie's favourite among Eric's books. Obviously they had been given the wrong rooms. Allie had found only a striped frog swimming round her lavatory bowl, and scooped it out with the red

139

plastic jug which presumably had been supplied for the purpose.

'I'll swap rooms if you like,' she offered, pulling Tasha past the man who had stepped out from his shop, a structure hung with carpets and fabrics and fronted by a rail of sun-faded garments.

'But I really need a sarong,' Tasha protested, adding, 'no, it's OK, he's quite a sweet gecko. We've bonded.'

There were no pebbles on the beach, just shells and slivers and tiny glittering particles in the process of being ground into sifting sand. The fishing fleet floated along the horizon. Pineapple tops pecked by the crows and hollow coconuts were the only litter. Tasha picked up two coconut shells, doing a little dance and singing 'At the Copa, Copacabana'. Allie was reminded of the sinister, sinuous beach boys who writhed around Ava Gardner in *The Night of the Iguana*; Deborah Kerr arriving in her white dress at that ramshackle clifftop hotel and Richard Burton as Shannon, the whisky priest tied to his hammock like the poor tethered iguana.

'Look at this!' she exclaimed, running her fingers along the heavy, hewn flank of an upturned boat as they undressed in its shadow. 'Just think, Tasha — generations of fishermen have been putting out to sea in craft of this self-same design, if not in this very vessel, from time immemorial.' A lump came to her throat as she said, 'You know that poem by

Flecker, "The Old Ships" …'

'Not that I recall', said Tasha. 'Personally, I think dropping the poetry list was the best thing we ever did.'

They waded into the warm sea, which flounced around their legs. Tasha flung herself on to a wave. Unfortunately, this crazy granny spouting on about poetry was the price she had to pay for February in Goa. She was in no doubt that if they should happen on Allie's fugitive author, it would be her and not Allie that he would fall for. Anyway, old Alabaster would be a wizened wreck by now, out of his head on toddy, palm wine and drugs. Allie wasn't bad for her age though, she had to concede; tall, naturally thin and fair, divorced a hundred years ago. She never spoke about her private life and Tasha supposed she didn't have one, apart from her family, which didn't count. Tasha swam out a bit further and turned to wave. Allie stood gazing at the horizon, with the modest skirt of her swimming costume undulating gently on the surface like a jellyfish.

Allie was thinking about her grandchildren, little Alf and Rosy, setting them down with their buckets and spades in what shade the palm trees gave, anointing them with total sunblock, arranging the folds of candy-coloured Foreign Legion caps to protect their tender, hollowed necks, showing them the antennae waving from a spiral shell. She waved back to the bikini-ed philistine sporting on the crest of a wave and swam out to join her. It was absurd to be blubbering over her grandchildren when she was here, in a Shangri-La far too hot for them, on a quest that might crown her career.

Allie and Tasha were sitting under the woven palm-leaf roof of one of the restaurants strung along the sands, sipping pineapple lassi, with boldly patterned sarongs draped round their shoulders and two more in their beach bags. 'Might as well stick with the pineapple,' Allie had said. When they had emerged from the sea, six or seven hawkers were camped beside their clothes, one of them a young girl with a basket of fresh fruit on her head. Half-naked among the swelling crowd of brightly clothed, bejewelled traders and basted by the sun, they were a pair of pink sitting ducks. Sticky with pineapple juice and clutching their purchases, they had fled ignominiously at last from the wheedling, bullying voices.

'You must admit it has a mellow tone', said Tasha, stroking a note from the drum on her knees. 'And your sandalwood beads do smell divine.'

'I'll probably give them to my daughter, Sal.'

Allie showed the boy who brought their drinks her copy of *The Gecko* with Eric's picture on its cover, but drew a blank.

'I had a word with Madame Da Silva. I've arranged for us to hire a couple of bikes tomorrow. We can make an early start into the interior,' she told Tasha.

'But I've rented a scooter from him. Mister Da Silva. I thought you could ride pillion.'

'Absolutely not. I've paid the deposit. Anyway, you don't have a licence.'

'You don't need one here. I paid a deposit too – anyway, I thought you'd be pleased that I'd used my initiative, like you're always telling me to.'

'We're not in the office now, Tasha. You'll just have to explain and get your money back.'

Tasha's straw siphoned up a piece of pineapple with a mutinous gurgle.

'I suppose you do realize', she said, 'that there are probably dozens of ancient, white-haired, superannuated hippies in Goa. Perhaps that's your bloke walking along the beach, mahogany man there with the medallion and ponytail.'

We must remain friends at least for the duration, Allie thought. Then we shall see how warm that expensive Pashmina keeps our young friend when she gets back to London and finds herself out on her ear, busking in the underground with her drum.

'Just think how all that pedalling will tone up our thighs. And walking on the sand and swimming, it'll do us more good than weeks at the gym,' she said.

Tasha stretched out a leg as if she could see no room for improvement in that taut calf.

They dined at another beach café on a table sunk in sand. The delicately spiced food was delicious. How pretty the blue fairylights looping the fronded canopy were, like blue chillies hung out to dry in the warm wind, how clear the stars. How desolate Allie felt. Ghostly crabs scurried from the sea's lacy edge and disappeared in the darkness of the beach. If only it were Eric sitting here beside her, his hand over hers. Tasha was flirting with a dog.

What a waste, thought Tasha.

In a concerted effort at amusement they giggled at the dessert menu. Buddha's Belly. A Goanese speciality. They insisted they must try it. Slivers of striated cake decked with cream and star fruit.

'Strange but surprisingly good,' said Allie.

Tasha agreed. If Allie imagined she was going to spend every evening chortling over Buddha's Belly with her, she had another think coming. A couple strolled hand in hand along the beach. Allie became aware that she was humming 'Hello, Young Lovers' from *The King and I*. So it had come to this.

'It's been a long day. Shall we go back now?' she asked. At least Tasha wouldn't have recognized the song; everything before 1960 was pre-history as far as she was concerned.

'It's ten to nine.'

Allie sat it out for the duration of another drink before saying that she really had to get to bed.

'OK,' said Tasha, but when they came to Fernandez

Hideaway, the last bar on the beach before the track that led to Da Silva's, she sat down at a table, saying, 'You go ahead. I'll see you in the morning.'

'I can't leave you here by yourself. It's really dark.'

'Don't be ridiculous. I'm a big girl.'

'No you're not.'

But she left her under the awning to the beat of a 1980s hit, and worried as she lay on her bed beneath the whirring ceiling fan, writing postcards, not tired in the least. She addressed the postcard of the Taj Mahal to her mother. Tasha captured by dacoits, Tasha wandering on the deserted beach, scantily dressed, Tasha the streetwise Londoner following some local Lothario into the darkness beyond the banyan trees to find herself lassoed by a liana and surrounded by jeering youths, unable to defend herself. Allie took her chair outside to watch the stars, and was disconcerted to see a security guard, a *chowkidar* in a quasi-military uniform patrolling the grounds with a rifle. She could hear the sea, and through the open windows of Number Four, the unmistakable sounds of the honey-mooners making love. She went in again, locking her door and putting the key on her bedside table.

She was woken by a raucous massed choir of crows. Sunshine was streaming through her shutters. She showered, put on a white cotton dress, and went out on to her veranda.

145

'Morning!'

A middle-aged English couple in crisp shirts and shorts were eating Weetabix outside Number One.

'Your daughter beat you to it, then,' said the man.

'I'm sorry?'

'Off out on her scooter half an hour ago. What it is to be young, eh?'

All Allie could say was, 'Where did you get your coffee?'

'Kitchen,' said the woman. 'Why don't you trot along and get yours and join us for breakfast. You're welcome to some of our Weetabix — we always travel with a few boxes just in case, and Jonty won't set foot in Abroad without his Marmite.'

'Thanks', said Allie faintly. She recognized them then as the popular thespians Jilly and Jonty Hazlecombe, stars of a dozen indistinguishable TV sitcoms. He played the irascible husband, she the long-suffering wife.

'Blasted milk's hot again,' said Jonty, peering into the aluminium jug. 'Can't these people ever get it right? Is the concept of cold milk quite beyond their powers of reasoning?'

'Give it to me, I'll take it back,' said Jilly patiently. 'I'll walk along with — sorry, what did you say your name was? We're Jonty and Jilly, by the way.'

'Alicia. I know you are — I mean, I recognized you of course.'

They left Jonty musing aloud, 'Alicia. We knew an Alicia once. Darlington rep, 1972, was it, darling?'

As Allie followed Jilly to the Da Silvas' kitchen, blinking away the tears caused by Tasha's latest betrayal, she reflected that, having recently read a magazine feature on the Hazlecombes, she knew rather more than she wished to about Jilly and Jonty's home life. The walls of their eighteenth-century coach house, with its superb view of the Thames, were crowded with the naïve Victorian portraits of pigs that they loved to pick up at antiques fairs or while pottering round junk shops. Jonty was partial to a particular black pudding that could be obtained only from a specialist butcher in Barnes; Sunday mornings often found Jonty in the couple's recently refurbished French farmhouse-style kitchen, enjoying 'cook's perks' of some fine château-bottled vintage as he experimented with the latest exotic recipe cajoled from a local chef while on a well-earned holiday off the beaten track. Jilly's tapestry chair backs, stitched during quiet moments between takes, were a byword among their host of theatrical friends. The Hazlecombe children, Ferdinand and Perdita, had followed their parents into the profession. Allie had seen them both recently, Ferdi and Perdi, now in their twenties, playing mildly mutinous teenagers in a middle-class drama she had been too lethargic to switch off.

Over coffee she found herself confiding her quest to the

Hazlecombes and showing them Eric Alabaster's picture. Jonty prodded it with his finger.

'I'm pretty sure we spotted your chappie the other day. Along the coast at Benaulim. Hair down to his shoulders, wearing one of those thong thingies and nothing else. Haggling over a pineapple with half a dozen beach boys.'

'He was a German paedophile, darling!'

The Hazlecombes paused, as if listening for the canned laughter which did not follow their exchange.

'We're booked on the dolphin trip at nine. I'm sure they could squeeze another one in if you're up for it,' said Jilly.

'As the actress said to the bishop,' said Jonty.

'Maybe not this morning,' Allie said. 'I'd better wait for Tasha. We've rented a couple of pushbikes.'

When she saw dolphins it would not be courtesy of the Hazlecombes, jammed up against Jonty's hairless leg with its sea anemone of broken veins.

'Have fun then,' said Jonty, with a petulant quiver of his full lower lip.

Then he was on his feet, bending forward with one leg cocked behind him, left hand palm upwards on the base of his spine, right hand shielding his eyes as he scanned the horizon,

'"Has anybody seen our ship?"' he sang. '"The HMS –"'

'Dis-gusting,' supplied Jilly, breaking into a few steps of a sailor's hornpipe.

Allie remembered that they had returned to their first love, the stage, a few months ago to star in a brief season of Noël Coward's shorter works at a provincial theatre, for charity.

Eleven o'clock found Allie pedalling along with sea water spurting from her tyres, avoiding jellyfish and minute crabs that disappeared down tiny tunnels. She saw a sun-dried red chilli floating in a frill of foam. It was exhilarating, but she knew that at some point she must dismount and push the bike through the soft sand to the road and peer into people's yards and through their windows. How much easier it would be if Tasha were there. Allie had no doubt that Tasha had sped off to some assignation made last night under the coloured light bulbs of Fernandez Hideaway. In spite of herself, she smiled at the sandpipers running from her on their twinkling legs; she rested to watch them and a dozen men who were burned to the colour of the boat they were hauling ashore. Then at the approach of a group of women with bulging bags, each holding out a sarong to catch the breeze, gaudy billowing ships in full sail, Allie mounted her saddle and accelerated away.

On the road she encountered pairs of pink Brits on bicycles, local people going about their business, a herd of buffalo, huge velvet-winged butterflies that she tried to capture on her camera. A group of schoolgirls called out to her and Allie braked in the dust. They wanted pens, she realized too late. Had she known before she embarked on this trip how often she would meet this request she would have armed herself with a hundred plastic Bics. Ashamed of her penless state, but with her heart beating faster as she took her copy of Eric's *Angostura Bitters* from her bag, she searched each face for a trace of English paternity. The girls assumed the book was a gift, took it disdainfully, and walked on. At a roadside clothes stall Allie stopped again and pushed through the flap of carpet which draped its interior. Twenty minutes later she came out into the glare none the wiser about Eric but in possession of a grey embroidered skirt and blouse. Streaks of colour in the folds suggested they had once been blue. Sitting on a iron chair at a Coca-Cola stand, watching an ancient woman scratching red soil with a wooden rake, Allie was conscious of being thousands of miles from home and in someone else's country.

She cycled on until she came to a blindingly white church like an elaborate bridal cake with many coats of royal icing starting to melt in the sun. If anybody could tell her if Eric Alabaster was in this part of the country, it would be the parish priest. The church was empty. Bunches of flowers wilting on the ends of the pews were redolent of a recent wedding. Allie lit a candle, mumbling an embarrassed anglican request to Saints Anthony and Jude to help her to find Eric, hoping that a fatherly old priest would emerge from one of the confessionals and perceive her as not just another vulgar tourist. She lingered in front of a painting of St Francis Xavier, with her new skirt draped over her head as a sign of respect, but no priest came.

'You might have waited!' Tasha was sprawled topless in a chair outside her apartment. 'Don't tell me you actually paid money for that faded ethnic tourist tat after all you've said! They must have seen you coming.'

'Cover yourself up! What would the Da Silvas think? Remember you're in a Catholic country.'

'That's OK, I'm a Catholic.'

Tasha's insolent breasts jeered at her, provoking her to say, 'Look, Tasha, let's not keep up the pretence that we're colleagues or even friends. As far as I'm concerned you're at perfect liberty to do anything you like. Go off with whom you like, get murdered by anyone you choose. It's fine by me.'

A sudden jagged pain seemed to split her skull, making her think of a tree struck by lightning. Holding her head in both hands she staggered into her room to lie down on the bed. Above her the ceiling fan whirled like a giant mosquito. She closed her eyes, realizing that she stayed out too long in the sun.

Allie woke in darkness and was at once conscious of a raging thirst. The bottle of mineral water in her bathroom was empty. The frog was back, gazing at her from the closed lid of the lavatory. Tasha, she remembered, had bought several bottles of water from Madame Da Silva. The stars were low and bright as she walked the few steps to Tasha's room. When she pushed open the door she thought at first she had come into the honeymooners' apartment by mistake until she saw that it was Tasha sitting up in bed with the *chowkidar* she had seen last night. He was wearing his cap. His rifle lay across the sheet.

'Why are you always barging in where you're not wanted?' demanded Tasha.

'I'm sorry. I was only looking for some water.'

There was a tray on the floor, with dirty cereal bowls and a crushed plastic bottle. Beside it stood a large jar of Marmite.

'That's Jonty's Marmite! How could you, Tasha? And it's crawling with ants!'

Then she screamed. The gecko was cowering in a corner with a rope noose round its neck. It was much bigger than Allie had imagined, with its jaws open in a rictus of panic and spotted sides heaving. The gecko snarled at her, shooting out a forked tongue as she approached.

'Don't bite. I'm your friend. I've come to save you,' Allie whispered as she managed to grasp a frayed end of rope.

'Oi! Put that back, it's for our barbecue later!' Tasha shouted. 'Stop her, Xavier! Kill her!'

A shot whizzed past Allie's head as she dragged the gecko across the stone floor and into the night. She touched her hair and felt sticky blood as she ran.

The palm tree fans were opening and shutting in the wind, rattling their spines like porcupines' quills. Banyan trunks swayed and swerved, blocking the path as she lurched on in terror, clutching at her with fibrous tentacles. She could hear branches cracking underfoot as Tasha and Xavier pursued her, and screamed when a crow swooped into her face, battering her with black wings. A snake lashed at her from a liana; she saw that all the creepers were alive with snakes, coiled ready to spring and baring phosphorescent fangs. Now the gecko was hauling her into the undergrowth, bounding up the steps of a shuttered house and into a brightly lit room full of people. Safe. Thank God. She heard the rhythmic shuffle of maracas and her knees buckled as she saw Tasha gyrating topless to the beat of the drum that Xavier held between his knees. The claws of a crab waved from the muzzle of his rifle on the floor.

Jilly Hazlecombe seized her arm, saying, 'I thought you were never coming.'

'As the actress said to the bishop,' said Jonty. They were dressed in matching white sailor suits.

'Run along to make-up,' Jilly shook Allie hard, her eyes hard with contempt. 'You're on in five minutes. *Red Peppers* might be just a great big joke to you, but this is a charity performance and there's an audience out there entitled to a bit of professionalism.'

Before Allie could protest, the gecko pulled her over to the corner. Eric Alabaster lay in a low-slung hammock sipping liquor from a coconut, through a straw. A clerical collar hung crookedly round his neck.

'Eric! I've found you!' Allie felt tears running down her face. 'I've been looking everywhere for you! But I didn't know you were a priest! Why weren't you in the church?'

'I'm a whisky priest now. They locked me out of my church.'

He petted the head of the gecko, which was nuzzling up to him, planting huge front feet on his chest and licking his face. As Allie watched, its skin tone flushed through dingy brown to a vivid emerald green with purple spots.

'I never thought you of all people would be so cruel as to tie up a wild iguana, Alicia,' Eric said.

'But I didn't! I rescued him from Tasha and Xavier. They were going to barbecue him. I've come to save you too, Eric. I love you. I've come to take you back to London with me, where you belong. I didn't know it until recently but I've been missing you all my life. We'll always be together now, and I've got such plans for relaunching all your books – and you, my darling. Look, the iguana's changing colour like a chameleon. That shows he's happy now.'

Kneeling beside the hammock, she stroked Eric's bleached hair.

'Come to the beach with me. There's something I want to show you,' said Eric, swinging his legs to the floor and cutting the rope from the iguana's neck.

He had his arm round her waist and as they walked Allie could feel her leg pressing against his. At the sea's edge he stooped and picked up a stick. ERIC ALABASTER, he wrote in large letters in the sand, and laughed as the sea obliterated his name.

'No!' cried Allie, grabbing at the stick.

Eric pushed her roughly to the sand, forcing the coconut shell of whisky to her mouth, scratching her face with its whiskery edges.

'Drink, damn you. You don't fool me, coming on like Deborah Kerr in your virginal white dress.'

When Tasha had knocked on Allie's door and got no reply she had assumed that she was asleep or sulking. Eventually, feeling hungry, she had taken the scooter and ridden a few miles inland to Rodriguez Bar and Restaurant, where she had enjoyed a drink earlier with one of the Da Silva sons. Before she could be joined by anybody more interesting, the Hazlecombes debouched from a taxi and invaded her table to regale her with an account of the dolphin trip. Nobody had drowned or been eaten by a shark; it seemed to Tasha very dull fare. To be stuck with the English abroad was her idea of hell; at least, unlike Allie, she had made an effort to get to know the locals.

'Have you ever thought of writing your memoirs?' she asked vengefully. 'You should have a word with Allie about it.'

When there was still no response from Allie the following morning, Tasha became alarmed and enlisted the help of Jilly and Jonty. They fetched Madame Da Silva with her key. Allie was in a sweaty heap on the bed, still in her cotton dress, all twisted in the sheet.

'She's burning up' said Jonty. 'Get some water.'

Tasha brought a bottle from her apartment. Jilly held it to Allie's mouth, letting the water dribble down her chin on to her chest. Allie writhed, blindly pushing the bottle away, choking.

'Don't try to speak, lovey. Just drink. You've gone and got yourself all dehydrated.'

Allie sat up. Her head was throbbing and her skin felt tight and sore. Jilly's cool hand was stroking the wet hair back from her forehead, holding not a coconut shell but a bottle of mineral water to her lips. Tasha and Jonty were there and Madame Da Silva.

'Well, you gave us all a scare!' said Jonty.

'You certainly did. How could you be so stupid as to go racing around on a bike in the sun all day like that? I don't suppose it occurred to you that you'd ruin my holiday too if you made yourself really ill,' said Tasha.

'There, there,' said Jilly. 'Tasha's just having a reaction. It's the relief,' she explained to Allie. 'You're going to be fine. I've got some pills you can take.'

'No thank you,' said Allie. 'Some people take a drink, others take a pill. I just take a few deep breaths. Or I would if I were Deborah Kerr in *The Night of the Iguana*. Which apparently I'm not.'

In a remnant of dream the green and purple spotted iguana deflated like a child's beach toy into a wrinkled balloon lifted by a wave.

'Stay in the shade for a day or two and you'll be as right as rain, eh Madame?' Jonty advised. Madame Da Silva nodded.

'I'll bring you some tea,' she said.

Right as rain, thought Allie. I want rain. I want to go home. She saw the corner of a damp English park and a child on a swing soaring through an arc of grey air, her own arms extended to push it higher, over loamy mud silvered by racing clouds, a snatch of hazel catkins, a blur of pale sulphur pussy willow; her hands reaching out to catch the swing and bring it safely down.

'That's right, a nice cup of tea. You get some rest and then you can carry on with your quest for your writer chappie when you're feeling up to it,' said Jilly.

'No,' said Allie. 'Eric Alabaster doesn't want to be found. I realize that now.'

'Well,' Jilly said. 'We're off to the flea market at Anjuna but we'll pop back to check on you later. Jonty's got a proposition to put to you. In your professional capacity, of course.'

'As the bishop said to the actress,' said Jonty.

Barbarians

When Ian and Barbara Donaldson started the mail-order children's clothes company Barbarians, operating from the family home in one of those parts of London that thinks itself a village, their own brood of four modelled Barbara's designs. As the business expanded, the offspring of some of their home workers were co-opted, to bring a bit of light and shade to the catalogue, and despite Barbara's initial *faux pas* of forcing a little Sikh boy with his hair in a mobcap into a dress with matching tights, the results were so charming that the orders flowed in and Ian was negotiating the purchase of new factory premises. The Donaldson boys' hair was cut in shiny pudding-basin style and ranged in tones from conker brown, through sun-streaked blond to white; it was Amber, the oldest at eleven, who was the problem. As her mother often remarked, Amber had been born on a bad-hair day, and now, with her string-coloured frizz scraped back in a scrunchie, scowling through the Cutler and Gross frames that didn't help much, she stuck out in the photographs like a sore thumb. She often *had* a sore thumb, or a bandage or Elastoplast somewhere about her person, and managed to look like a refugee in the snazziest Barbarian togs.

'We're supposed to be promoting "Fun Fashions for Real Kids", not soliciting donations for some Third World charity,' Ian complained, slapping down a pile of prints on the table in the breakfast room, where he and Barbara were lingering over coffee and brioches at eleven o'clock on a spring half-term Tuesday morning, having decided not to go down to their Suffolk cottage. Ian was a big, jovial man, ruddy-faced with white curls tumbling on to the collar of his denim shirt and springing through the gaps between the buttons. Holidays in the French farmhouse they were renovating had taught him to prefer his chips fried in horse fat and he was spearheading a campaign to get Dobbie's, the local butchers, to stock it.

'But Amber *is* a real kid,' her mother felt obliged to point out, then conceded, 'poor lamb, she's not quite Barbarian, is she, bless her little cotton socks.'

She shook her head over the photographs, rattling the beads that had been plaited into her fair hair on a recent buying trip to the Caribbean. She had an emergency appointment at the hairdresser's that afternoon to have them cut out.

'Daddy.' Amber came into the room with her friend Rukhsana in tow. Her yellow cotton socks flopped, as if there was no Lycra in them at all. 'Daddy,' she demanded, 'do you believe in a minimum wage policy?'

'I do not, Pop Tart, and I'll tell you for why. Sit yourself down, and have some juice. *Et tu, ma petite Rucksack, un jus de pomme pour toi aussi, hein?*'

Rukhsana giggled dutifully as Ian poured from the bottle labelled Château Donaldson. His favourite daydream was of a *fête champêtre* beneath the blossom, with all his family, including his two ex-wives, their children and assorted partners, seated at a long table in the orchard, and himself at the head, standing to carve. Babies toddled through the daisies and crawled under the white cloth that was weighted with meats, fishes, fruit, cheeses, green walnuts, jugs of young wine and cobwebbed bottles of the finest vintage, platters piled with bones and rinds and shells; and at last, as the first stars pricked the evening sky, an enormous cake was carried in triumph over the darkening dewy grass, tremulous with the flames of sixty candles.

'Well, Daddy?' said Amber.

'I do not support the theory of the minimum wage for two reasons, Pop Tart. The first being that it is simply unworkable, and the second that enforcement of such a policy in a market economy would mean that your papa would be unable to employ such estimable ladies as our young friend here's delightful mama, and what would poor Rucksack do then, poor thing, and all her little brothers and sisters, eh? You wouldn't want to see your friends out on the street, would you? And your old mum and dad in the debtors' prison?'

'But, Dad, it doesn't seem fair that we –'

'That's enough, Amber!' Barbara cut her off. 'Your

father's explained. Go and find Marie-Claude and see if she needs any help with the boys. And Amber, do please change into a Mood Indigo Tee with those saffron leggings. If I've told you once, that range is mix'n'match! Do *try* to remember that you are an ambassador for Barbarians at all times.'

Amber slammed down her glass, and the girls left the room just as Barbara was saying to Ian, 'Saffron can be so draining on a sallow skin.'

'That's all I need, my own kid turning into a barrack-room lawyer. She'll be manning a picket line outside the front gate next. Little Roxanne's getting to be quite a looker though, isn't she? I suppose they'll be finding a husband for her soon.'

'Don't be so ridiculous, Ian. The child's still in primary school,' snapped Barbara, scratching her thigh, where a line of sunburn marked the hem of her beach shorts. Beneath her clothes she was as pink and white as a Battenberg cake, and starting to peel.

As they went upstairs, Rukhsana asked, 'Why does your dad call you Pop Tart?'

'Same reason as he calls you Rucksack, because he's a dickhead.'

Amber's bedroom smelled mustily of the mice who lived in Mouse Palace, the brightly coloured perspex construction that sat on top of her bookcase like a miniature Pompidou Centre. These piebald pets served two purposes: Amber adored them, and they kept Marie-Claude out of her room, as well as Barbara, who could tolerate rodents only when they were made of felt and dressed in Victorian clothes. Amber and her brother Diggory, the next in line, had a contract; he would not let Willow the cat in as long as she refrained from popping the blisters on his collection of bubble wrap.

'You're sad you know, Diggory. It's like you really love that stuff. I mean, I wouldn't keep clingfilm for a pet, would I?' Rukhsana told him once. Then she went on to cajole, 'Let me pop one, just one, go on Digg, *please, please, please.* I'll give you a whole packet of Jolly Ranchers for just one pop.'

Diggory shook his head, smiling and backing away with a roll of bubble wrap clutched to his chest. 'Get a life, Diggory,' said Rukhsana in disgust.

Now, the voices of the two younger boys and Marie-Claude, who was the daughter of the schoolmaster in the village where the Donaldsons had bought their farmhouse, came plaintively from the garden, which backed on to a small wood. Beyond that was the railway line which carried commuter trains, Eurostar and nuclear waste along the edge of the Donaldsons' lives; in summer the line was screened by the leaves of the trees which were now putting out a fuzz of catkins and buds. The children were forbidden to play in the

Coppice, as the wood had been named by a local estate agent — Ian called it the Codpiece — and so naturally they had a secret entrance through the fence to the fox-runs and the railway bank.

'What do you want to do?' Amber asked. 'Shall we watch a video of *Ab Fab*?'

The two girls were word-perfect, even though Rukhsana had not been allowed to watch the series at home. They sprawled on cushions on the floor, spitting crisp crumbs as they laughed, oblivious to Siobhan the cleaner, who came in to vacuum listlessly around them.

Ian had been married to Nell, his second wife and the mother of his twins, when Barbara, then a fashion student on vacation, came to work as a waitress in the restaurant they were running. Ian moved in with Barbara as soon as she graduated. Nell changed the name of the restaurant from Le Boeuf sur le Toit to Déjeuner sur l'Herbe, and was operating it still, as a successful wholefood café, while Daniel and Damien were building a reputation as chefs elsewhere. They came into Barbara's mind, duelling gracefully with a pair of knife-sharpeners, as she leafed through the Divertimenti catalogue, accepting regretfully that there was no piece of equipment, however desirable, that her own kitchen really needed. Once Barbara had enjoyed fiction and biographies, but now her bedside table was piled with magazines, brochures and catalogues even though she rationed the children's comics and had claimed to have sleepless nights over Jack's refusal to read at seven and a half. She looked at the clock and groaned.

'Is that really the time? Half-term is so disorientating; we might as well have gone down to the cottage. Be a love and get Wills for me, would you?'

'OK, *mon ange*. I'd better get on the road. Don't wait lunch,' said Ian, and was through the door, roaring 'Wills!', before Barbara could ask where he was going. She felt the premonition of a headache and wondered if it was those damn beads weighing her down.

When Amber came into the garden room, she found her mother lying on the sofa with her eyes closed and Wills on his little milking-stool, glued to a *Thomas the Tank Engine* video.

'What do you want now?' Barbara snarled. 'You know this is my Quality Time with Wills.'

Amber went out through the french windows, waiting until she was in the garden before she said, 'Who needs a Fat Controller with her around?'

Marie-Claude was hunched on the seat of the swing, rubbing her eyes with a tissue, while Diggory pushed.

'I bet if we both pushed really, really hard, we could push

her all the way over the rooftops, up into the sky, all the way back to *la belle France*,' said Amber.

Ian, having left Barbara without explanation, was in a Portuguese café a couple of miles from home, drinking an espresso while he waited at a corner table for two. Sunshine freckled the floor and chrome and glass and the display case of spun-sugar storks and cradles for christening cakes. Two old men sat playing chess and mothers with *bambini*, or whatever they called them, came in to buy bread and choose from the array of cakes and *pasteis de nanta*. Ian stretched his legs contentedly in his little patch of Abroad, kicking the table next to him.

'Do you mind?'

'I beg your pardon, madam.'

Ian saw a woman, invisible until now, glaring at him as he apologized. She was a skinny, faded blonde, intrusively English, wearing a grey sweatshirt over leggings. She lit a cigarette, and coughed, one of those neurotic crones who smoke themselves to death and then expect the NHS to provide a bed for them to die in. No wonder the country was in such a state, with an ever-increasing population of no-hopers draining its resources from the cradle to the grave. Ian could see it all, the funeral procession holding up the traffic with its sanctimonious floral tributes spelling out MUM and NAN. There was something vaguely familiar about the woman and he wondered if she had worked for him in some capacity. She had one of those red, white and blue striped shopping bags, which common people take to the supermarket or launderette. He hoped that she was not going to claim acquaintance with him, and closed his eyes to let the Portuguese music drift over him.

He opened them as a chair was scraped back and the table wobbled, and he half-rose with a smile as Laura sat down. She was eighteen, training to be a nurse and had filled in as a mother's help between the departure of the Donaldsons' last nanny and the arrival of Marie-Claude.

'I'm late,' she said.

'Only ten minutes. It couldn't matter less, sweetie, only I am a bit pushed. Cappuccino, and how about one of those delicious-looking cakes? I'm going to, although I know I shouldn't. Cholesterol nightmare, what?'

Ian went up to the counter and ordered coffee and a cream horn oozing custard and a glistening layered confection decorated with swirls of red and yellow.

'I feel like a naughty schoolboy playing truant,' he said setting down the tray. 'Reminds me of my prep school days. Tuck in, and then we'll hotfoot it back to yours.' He glanced at his watch. 'I take it Mum's safely out of the way?'

'I mean, I'm late. You know, late! As in overdue.'

Froth spilled into the saucer as Ian sat down, feeling desire draining away. Those words again. One more woman's stricken face staring at his. There was something embarrassingly old-fashioned about the scenario.

'Are you sure? I mean, couldn't you have miscalculated?' He knew his lines.

Laura shook her head. Her hair was dragged into a ponytail, and she wore no make-up. Funny how women adopt the least-becoming hairstyles when they're out to trap a bloke. Bad tactics.

'It's nearly two weeks.'

'Oh well, a fortnight's nothing. That eating disorder you told me about probably buggered up your cycle. Here, eat your cake like a good girl and stop worrying.'

'That was ages ago.' Laura pushed away the tray. 'If you'd bothered to ask, I only wanted a glass of water.'

'Oh, for God's sake.' Ian stuck a fork into the cake. 'How could you have been so stupid as to take a risk? I thought –'

'It takes two to tango,' put in the woman at the next table.

Ian turned on her, 'Who asked your opinion? What bloody business is it of yours and what makes you think you have the right to eavesdrop and butt in on a private conversation?'

'This is my mum. Mrs Kelly,' said Laura. 'Mum, Mr Donaldson.'

'I said, it takes two to tango,' repeated Mrs Kelly, ignoring her daughter's introduction.

Ian thumped the table in disbelief and fury at being set up.

'Madam,' he said, 'it may well take two to tango, as you so originally put it, but what makes you think I was your daughter's only dancing partner?'

'You bastard.' Laura burst into tears.

Ian shoved the table out of his way and blundered towards the door.

'You haven't heard the last of this. Not by a long chalk!' Mrs Kelly's voice pursued him. 'Sitting there like Lord Muck, with cream on your chin and your high-and-mighty talk of cycles and prep school ... and who's paying for this lot, eh? My daughter never ordered those pastries.'

'The woman always pays, that's what they say, isn't it?' Ian slammed the café door behind him.

He regretted his words as soon as he was back in the car; it had probably been a dangerous mistake to outsmart the stupid mare. He leaned across to look in the vanity mirror. Ma Kelly had been right about the cream. Ian watched his tongue licking his chin, and saw one eye closing in a wink that said, 'Uh-oh, who's been a bad lad, then? Playing away from home again eh, you old devil.'

Responding with a rueful grin, he started the engine. There might be life in the old dog yet, but he had broken the eleventh commandment: Thou shalt not be found out.

'Any calls while I was out?' Ian asked Amber when he got home.

'Only Granny Molly. She's coming on Sunday. There's an antiques fair at the college and she says I can go with her.'

Amber gave an irritating skip of pleasure. Piggotts College, Ian's alma mater, one of London's oldest public schools, stood in its park ten minutes' walk away. The two older boys attended Piggotts prep and Wills was at the nursery. It annoyed Ian to imagine Molly poking through junk in the Great Hall.

'And me,' said Diggory. 'Granny Molly said I could come too.'

'Only because you begged,' Amber told him.

'Where's your mother? At the hairdresser?'

'She didn't go. She wasn't feeling well, so she cancelled her appointment. She's gone to lie down.'

Ian went upstairs. Jack was sitting against the wall outside the master bedroom, wrapped in his duvet.

'What on earth are you doing? Get up at once, you look like some homeless layabout in a shop doorway begging for change. Take that thing off and go and play in the garden, or read a book or do something useful. When I was your age, I'd have been ashamed to waste my half-term skulking in a quilt, sucking my thumb.'

'I want Mummy and she won't let me in. Anyway, you know I can't read.'

Ian was the first to look away. Jack's hazel eyes were defiant under his glossy fringe, his little legs in jeans drawn up to his chest. Oh well, if you have eight sons, perhaps it doesn't really matter that much if one of them is illiterate. Ian supposed it would sort itself out in time. He went into the bedroom. All that was visible of Barbara was a spray of beaded plaits on the pillow beside the sleeping cat.

'Where've you been?' her muffled voice accused.

'To the factory. I told you I had an appointment with the vendors. Sorry you're not feeling well, Pudding. I hope you didn't pick up some bug on that trip of yours. You've been looking a bit green round the gills since you got back.'

'Thanks. Don't bother to contact the Institute for Tropical Diseases yet, though. It's only a headache.'

'Try to get some rest, then. I'll bring you some tea in a bit.'

He found Jack still crouching outside. He had pulled the hood of his sweatshirt over his face.

Ian sighed. 'Come on then, Jackanory. I'm going to make Mums some tea later, and you can take it up. How's that?'

'Daddy?'

'My son?'

'*Have* you got any spare change?'

One of the many things that Ian held against his mother-in-law was that she was about his own age, but he resented more her indifference to his charm; even after giving her four grandchildren, and the success of Barbarians, Molly still managed to suggest that he was some sort of dilettante who could not be trusted with her daughter's happiness. Molly dealt in vintage clothes, 'rags' as she herself termed them, from a booth in an indoor antiques market in Highgate. Widowed when Barbara was a child of six, she had stayed true to the memory of her husband, which irritated Ian too; it seemed a waste and a reproach. He hated the smell and touch of old material, flaccid gauzy stuff, and velvets that set his teeth on edge and made him feel grubby. Most of all, he disliked Granny Molly's advocacy of Amber; she was always ready to leap to her defence, on the lookout for an imagined slight to her darling. Not that she didn't love the boys too, but her attitude to Amber implied some dereliction of duty on her parents' part; it was typical of Molly that it was she who had discovered that the kid needed glasses just before they realized she was short-sighted. None of his other kids wore specs. As far as Ian could see, Molly just sat in that arcade all day, sewing beads on old evening bags, smoking, gossiping and eating baked potatoes from the take-away upstairs. He decided to impress her with Sunday lunch *en famille*, and began planning the menu. It was ages since he'd made his Calvados apple tart.

Amber was in the kitchen, spooning flour into a bowl. Ian peered at the mixture. 'What's cooking, Pop Tart? More play dough for Wills? Tell him to try to keep it out of the carpet this time. Where's your better half?'

'If you must know, it's a practice run for my simnel cake. Rukhsana had to go home.'

'At least use a sieve for that flour then,' Ian said heavily. 'Here, Jackanory, there's a spoon for you. You can help your sister. You should take a leaf out of Rukhsana's book, Amber, and pay a bit more attention to your brothers. Leave the phone on answer, I'm not taking any calls.'

'As it happens, she's got to work. Her mum was up all night on the Easter order.'

When Ian had gone, Jack asked, 'What's a Jackanory mean?'

'It was a TV programme in the olden days. I expect he used to watch it with his other kids. Give me that, you're not sticking a licked spoon into my cake mixture.'

'I haven't even licked it yet. What's a sinimel cake?'

Amber looked at him. 'You're really going to have to get your act together, you know, Jack.'

Jack decided it must mean cinammon, and pulled down his hood again.

Merde, merde et trois fois merde, Ian thought, that's all I need, some kid buggering up the new range. The outworkers really were the end, letting their brats loose on the machines. No wonder they were constantly under repair. The sooner the factory was up and running the better. He switched on his computer to do a few sums, and paused to wonder what the going rate for a termination was these days and whether it could be done on plastic, then poured himself a shot of Calvados. Women. They'd be the ruination of him yet. Why was it his fate to attract the unfailingly fertile of the fair sex? Or was it perhaps a clever ruse on old Dame Nature's part, to equip the gene pool with superior breeding stock? God knows that was needed nowadays and he wouldn't be without his sprogs, any of them. He took another shot. Not excluding Amber, even if she was a poke-nosed clever-clogs who'd palled up out of contrariness with the wrong sort, instead of one of the more suitable girls from her own school; she might not have the looks he would have liked in his only daughter, but academically she knocked spots off the boys. Probably turn out to be more of an asset to the company than dreamy old Diggs, with his bubble wrap. Still, he supposed it showed the lad had a feel for texture. There was a piece of the stuff on his desk and Ian popped the blisters systematically, as if he were on a strand at low tide, bursting a ribbon of bladderwrack. A memory was niggling at him, of a woman with whom he'd had a casual fling some years ago. The telephone had rung while he'd been in the kitchen cooking for a dinner party.

'Ian, I've found a lump in my ...'

'And I've just found a lump in my béchamel. I'll call you back.'

He had rung her back, eventually, but she was dead.

Now he made himself focus on the Laura problem, but it

was all unthinkable and he couldn't face any of it. Scenes from various *ménages* flashed through his mind; women, children, ranks of largely forgotten in-laws and a procession of hamsters, stick insects, goldfish, cats. Pussy Cat Willum, Orlando, Kit Cat, Tigger, Bilbo Baggins. No, Bilbo Baggins had been a Volkswagen Beetle. Any incorporation of Laura, not to mention Mum Kelly with her sharp knees pointing through her leggings and black court shoes, into the picture was out of the question. He saw them sitting bitterly apart from the rest of the family, with a howling infant, turning the cream sour and the champagne flat at his *fête champêtre*. No, there was no way he could go through any of it again. Besides, Laura wasn't that much older than Amber; ought to be concentrating on her studies, the silly girl. Ian leaned back, lost in a reverie of Laura modelling the silk underwear he'd given her at Christmas. A smile softened his face, and he reached for the bottle. The ladies, God bless 'em!

Upstairs, Pussy Willow, bored, began to bat the beads on Barbara's pillow with his paw. She groaned. 'Leave me alone, you beast. Ouch, that was a claw! Get out of my hair. Why don't you go and catch a mouse or something?'

Barbara didn't need Willow to tell her the beads had been a mistake. The entire trip had been disastrous. Mercifully, Ian hadn't questioned her too closely, beyond remarking that she had brought back very little and he hoped the whole thing hadn't been an expensive waste of time.

'I admit Jamaica was a bit of a let-down, but these samples might turn out to be brilliant and I've made some very useful contacts. And that's partly what it's all about, isn't it?' she had told him. A length of bougainvillea-coloured cloth was churning round in the washing machine, on its third go, still pumping magenta dye into the system. Barbara had the Tropixie fashion shoot all planned; she was going to get a load of silver sand from a builders' merchant and have it tipped into the kids' old sandpit. She would stick in a branch of the hibiscus from the garden room and a palm frond or two from the florist. One of the women had a pair of divine twins, Taneesha and Tenara, who were so totally Tropixie that Barbara could just see them, with their hair in corn rows, and perhaps a blossom behind the ear, kneeling on either side of her own white-maned, blue-eyed palomino Wills, who, scrumptious as a vanilla ice, was smiling beatifically as he turned out a perfect sandcastle.

Queasily she turned over in bed, pushing away a coconut pierced by two straws, brimming with a foaming cocktail of guilt and longing. Her body was tingling and she was reminded of one of the children's toys, a magic wand, imported from God knew where and bought off a market stall. This transparent tube, tipped at either end with red plastic, was filled with a thousand floating rainbow specks and, although disappointingly powerless, was spellbinding in its mesmeric shiftings as it was turned first one way and then another. Barbara felt as if she had become that magic wand, weightless and swarming with polychromatic organisms, while pinpricks and flashes of light sparked the blackness behind her closed eyelids. Phosphorescent with desire, she had to deal with the knowledge that she had been unfaithful, and that she was lying in bed pretending to be ill. Perhaps she *was* ill, she hoped. Her head did ache and she was feverish.

One of the worst things she had to face was that Ian had been so proud of her going off on Barbarian business that he had bought her a new set of luggage, and all she'd done in return was drink too much rum punch with a bartender half her age, and grab a few rolls of cloth from the market on her way to the airport. They had been careful, Berris and she, as far as she could remember. With hindsight, she knew that Berris had forgotten her by now, that she had been the classic English dupe on holiday. It made her realize how much she loved Ian, but it caused her to wonder too how he could have borne the anxiety of infidelity so many times before he had found her. Recalling that he had just called her Pudding, his pet name for his former wives, made her feel a mite less anguish, although her heart beat too fast if she thought about their deception of Nell all those years ago, even if the end had justified the means, and now her own betrayal of Ian was doing her head in. Never, never again. A good wife and mother and business partner was what she would be from now on. But where was the tea Ian had promised her? She was so thirsty. Had he found out somehow? Where were the children? Why had they deserted her? Was Ian keeping them from her? Had she become a spectre in her own house, condemned to wander from room to room searching for them, in the blue beads of shame?

'Jack,' she called, 'you can come in now.'

There was no answer. She sweated and itched and peeled, not knowing what to do with herself, unable to find a comfortable position. She had never wanted to before, not in her wildest dreams, had thought herself incapable of such an act — making love with somebody younger and prettier than herself. Barbara writhed, sick with detestation of her charming, funny, beautiful young lover.

Molly was elated by the early blossom as she drove to her daughter's house. There is nothing in this world so lovely as London in the spring, she thought. It was almost nine o'clock, and the plan was that Molly should collect the two children and take them to the fair before the public was let in at eleven. She was looking forward to seeing Barbara and hearing all about her trip, and was prepared to feel benign towards Ian on this beautiful morning of church bells and daffodils and people looking cheerful in the sunshine. Even if he *was* a serial adulterer who would give you the derivation of the word denim at the drop of a hat; she, of all people, had nothing against second-hand goods or used merchandise, but a rorty, rollicking old foodie of a father-figure wasn't necessarily what you wanted for your only child. The thought of the children gave her pleasure too; Molly was in the privileged position of favourite grandparent, as Grandma and Grandpa Donaldson were pretty gaga now, and had long ago lost count of their grandchildren. Nevertheless, she often had to bite her tongue at the way the youngsters were being brought up, and she did feel intensely protective towards Amber. Molly was of the opinion that every child needs an adult who thinks she is the best thing since sliced bread, and she saw herself fulfilling that rôle for Amber, as if by taking it for granted that Amber was pretty and popular, she could make her so.

All the curtains were closed when Molly drew up outside the house. Diggory let her in, after the third ring.

'How's my best boy?' she asked, hugging him, catching a whiff of garlic on his breath.

'Everybody's still in bed, excepting me and Amber,' he told her.

'Have you had any breakfast?'

'Yes, we had some pitta bread and hummus.'

The house smelled of unopened windows and sleep. Amber came down the stairs, without her glasses on, looking pale and as vulnerable as one of her pet mice. Molly realized that not so long ago, Amber would have hurled herself into her arms, and said briskly, 'You'll need your specs, if you're going to be my picker.' She tapped her own frames in a businesslike way, and Diggory felt excluded.

'I hate them. I want to get contacts,' said Amber.

'I'm sure you will, when you're old enough. Let's get going, or all the decent stuff will be taken.'

Amber took her glasses from her pocket and put them on.

As they walked through the college gates, Molly looking vernal in her Balenciaga green linen dress and jacket, between the two unkempt and garlicky ambassadors for Barbarians, Amber said, 'Mum's not well. She picked up something on her trip, Dad thinks.'

'My mum went to the West Indies,' said Diggory.

'Jamaica?' Molly obliged.

'No, she went of her own accordion.'

Amber heaved a deep sigh.

'Diggory, do you have to get everything wrong? I think he does it deliberately, you know,' she said to Molly, woman to woman.

'Now, now,' said Molly. She almost said nobody likes a smart-ass, but asked, 'Tell me about poor Mum. How long has she been ill?'

'Only since yesterday, but she was hallucinating last night, I think. She was lying there going, "Too much loose dye, too

182

much loose dye," like the tailor of Gloucester when he went, "No more twist. No more twist."'

Ian was in the kitchen, wearing his butcher's apron and a chef's hat given to him by Daniel and Damien, when they returned. Diggory was clutching a roll of bubble wrap and Amber was sporting a garish Fifties' necklace. Molly had a couple of fusty-looking carrier bags. She stood on tiptoe to kiss Ian's jowls.

'Dad, if you knew what you looked like in that hat ...', said Amber.

Molly sighed. Ian, obviously hurt, said, 'Your slip's showing, Ma-in-law.'

Molly looked down. An edge of old lace was peeking from under her skirt. Annoyed, she said gaily, 'It's raining in Paris! That's what we used to say at school, didn't we, when somebody's petticoat was showing?'

'Not at Piggotts, we didn't,' Ian replied stiffly. She always had to rub it in that they were near contemporaries.

'How's Barbara? Should I go up and see her?'

'It's OK, I'm down. Hello Mum, good to see you. Hi, guys. Amber, where did that ghastly necklace come from? It really doesn't go with a hooded sweat.'

Molly saw her child, looking wan in a dressing gown, with touristy beads in her hair, and embraced her, winking at Amber, who had flinched.

'She's got an eye, you know. To some, that necklace is a collector's piece. Those braids are very amusing, but darling you look awful! Have you had the doctor?'

'No, I'm fine now. It was just one of those twenty-four-hour things. Probably something I ate.' She grimaced.

'I'm the one who deserves your sympathy, Molly. Tossing and turning all night, she was, sweating like the proverbial – if I didn't know better, I'd have thought she was having hot flushes. I didn't get a wink. Then the bloody foxes started their mating – sounded like a chainsaw massacre. I suppose they must enjoy it but –'

'Please, Ian, *pas devant les enfants* ...' Molly remembered how Ian used to line the children up and make them each say three rude words before breakfast, whether they wanted to or not. 'Gets it out of their system,' he would say.

'Oh, come on, Ma-in-law, there's nothing they haven't seen on those wildlife TV programmes. Probably know more about it than we do!' He took a slurp from a glass of white wine. 'Cook's perks. What can I get you, Molly? Barbie Doll? Up to a snort yet?'

'Perhaps a little wine, topped up with lots of mineral water,' Barbara said bravely.

'I'll have a G&T, thank you, Ian,' Molly said. 'Where are Jack and William? I haven't seen them yet.'

'They'll be with Marie-Claude.'

'I hate that smell, of meat when it's just starting to cook,' said Amber. 'Granny Molly, did you know I'm a vegetarian?' She picked a slice of apple from a dish and ate it.

'Ignore her, we do. She's just copying her little Asian friend,' Ian commented. 'Personally, I love it when the juices start to run. Gets my own juices running. Shall we take our drinks into the garden room? This will take some time. Amber, I hope you heard that apple scream when you bit into it?'

He took off his apron.

'You'd already killed it, stupid.'

Molly winced; she was so weary of being the referee. It would be immoral of course to wish the child would learn some feminine wiles, but she had to clench her fingers to stop them from removing the scrawny, scraggly — scrunchie, that was it — from Amber's hair.

Jack and Wills were in the garden room, watching television.

'How are my best boys?' cried Granny Molly. 'Still in their jimjams at nearly two o'clock? Where's Marie-Claude?'

'In the garden. All she ever does is sit on the swing and cry every time Eurostar goes past,' said Jack.

'Oorostar! Oorostar!' wailed Wills, and everybody laughed.

'I think she might be a bit homesick,' said Amber.

'We ought to try harder with her, Ian. I know she isn't easy, but she could blacken our characters to the whole *village, if she's unhappy.'*

'I have tried,' said Ian.

He thought suddenly, It's after two. There's been no word from Laura or her mum. No heavies have come looking for me. It must have been a false alarm. Thank you, God.

'Perhaps she's missing her horsemeat,' Amber suggested. 'Such a shame we can't get it at Dobbie's in the village.'

In the release from tension that washed over him, Ian exploded. 'Amber, I've had about as much as I can take from you with your constant sniping and undermining. If you despise us all so much, why don't you just pack your bags and go? And take your smelly mice with you! If you ever gave a thought to anybody but yourself, you'd get down on your knees every day and thank your mother and me. You don't know just how fortunate you are to live in a household like this. It's a jungle out there. You may sneer at my chef's hat, which of course you know has great sentimental value for me, but most of the kids you pass on the street have never watched their parents cook a proper meal, never seen them lift a needle or a hammer and chisel. They live on pot noodles and crack cocaine, savages in a new Dark Age, without hope, without pride, without skills. Is that what you want, eh? If it is, you can check out of that fancy school as soon as you like, and I won't waste any more thought or money on you. My God, those pampered pets of yours have a better lifestyle than half the world's population, how do you justify that? I doubt your friend Roxana has so much as a mousetrap to call her own, let alone a state-of-the-art mouse cage or an architect-designed bedroom to herself like you, but at least she does a bit of work to earn her keep. It's all take, take, take, gimme, gimme, gimme, with you, isn't it? You're not even any use to the catalogue, are you? Just a flaming liability!'

Barbara and Molly had both been attempting to remonstrate during this tirade as Ian delivered verbal blow after blow, but he was unstoppable. Throughout it, Amber had attempted to hold a supercilious expression, but the reference to a mousetrap broke her. She bolted for the door, her face twisted, eyes spouting angry, humiliated tears behind her glasses. Molly caught her and struggled to hold her tight.

'There, there, Daddy didn't mean it. Darling, don't fight me, don't cry, he didn't mean any of those things, you just rubbed him up the wrong way.' Molly was crying too. 'People say things they don't mean in the heat of the moment.'

'Of course, I didn't mean it, Amber knows I didn't mean it, don't you, Pop Tart? Silly old Daddy lost his rag back there for a minute, didn't he? Just got a bit stressed out because he's been under a lot of pressure. Come on, Pop Tart, give your old Popsicle a hug and tell him you forgive him, eh? Please? Pretty please!'

'Go on, darling. Kiss and make up, eh? Daddy's said he's sorry.'

Molly, kneeling with her arms round Amber, glared at her son-in-law's loins packed into denim, his trainers like two dead pigeons on the carpet, even as she pushed the girl forward.

'Yes, go on, sweetheart,' Barbara urged. 'Look the boys are crying, we're all crying. Let's stop all this silliness now.'

Ian fell to his knees now, pleading, striking his forehead with his fist. 'Forgive me, forgive me, or I shall surely die.'

Molly stood up, and Amber said, 'Dad, you are *so* embarrassing. OK, I forgive you. Even though I know you did mean every word. Just get up, all right?'

Amber walked towards him and Ian hoisted himself up to hug her. Amber avoided his kiss and, in a gesture that chilled her grandmother, held out a small, disdainful hand for him to shake.

'There, that's better. Now we can all forget all about it and get on with enjoying this lovely day,' said Granny Molly. 'Which of you boys is going to find Marie-Claude and bring her in to join us? Thank you, Diggory. Switch off the television and let's sit down like civilized people and have a conversation. Barbara, darling, when am I going to hear all your adventures? I'm all agog. Not now? Oh well, over lunch then, when you're feeling a bit more like yourself. Now, did anybody else see that very disturbing programme about the

child carpet weavers of Bhutan last night? No, perhaps not
… what pretty daffodils.'

'I picked them for Mummy because she was ill,' said Jack.

'They're lovely and they made Mummy better.' Barbara
blew her nose hard.

Molly lit a cigarette and walked over to the open french
windows. The garden was still wintry, except for one
forsythia, and bleached plastic vehicles were scattered in the
grass.

'You'll be able to get your first cut in soon, if this weather
holds,' she said to Ian, not without a touch of malice. Then
she saw, with a jolt to her heart, that the garden was quite
bare of daffodils, but the railway bank was ablaze with
them. Diggory was coming out of the Coppice, followed by
Marie-Claude. He was sucking the edge of a piece of bubble
wrap, and Molly recognized it for what it was, a comfort
blanket.

'Look, a magpie!' she exclaimed.

'Oh, there are masses around,' said Barbara. 'Loads more
than there used to be.'

'Roadkill,' said Ian. 'The increase of carrion has led to a
magpie population explosion. Breeding like rabbits, and
taking over the cities. There will have to be a cull soon,
they're decimating the local songbirds. Have you come
across that book, Ma-in-law, *The Roadkill Cookbook*? Some
surprisingly appetizing recipes.'

'Oh, good. A pair, that's lucky! Two for joy. And another!' said Molly.

'Three for a girl!' shouted Jack. 'Yuk. Where's four for a boy?'

Neither of his parents answered him.

The Last Sand Dance

After the taxi dropped him off, Alfred rode on beside her in a dark shape of Eau Sauvage and cigar smoke. Zinnia was driven south, with her eyes shut to retain his presence and her fingers closed on the note he had folded into her gloved palm to pay the cab, unsettled by his scent, once familiar and now exotic, and the impression of his heavy coat that she still held in her arms. The nylon spiracles of Zinnia's wide fur collar, electrified by the long-ago lovers' brief parting embrace, made an aureole round her small head like that of a red squirrel's tail against the light, and stirred her own hair into the tiny scarlet-tipped feathers of an African Grey parrot. It was late March, Passover and Easter just round the corner, and the clear moonlit night was cold enough to encourage a thin frost. She was on her way home from the theatre. When Alfred had telephoned to ask her to a play he had agreed to review for a quirky literary periodical, although his field was really Byzantine art, Zinnia had thought it might be a lark, especially as they had not seen each other since the funeral of a reprobate dramatist six months ago. The play, *Istambull*, had attracted rave notices at last year's Edinburgh Festival and won a Fringe First award.

Zinnia Herbert was an actor, with an unreconstructedly actressy West End glamour about her, even though she had not appeared on a stage north of Wimbledon for several years; Zinnia was one of those stalwarts who never quite become a star, whose kindness to their fellow thespians and the humblest ASM are legendary in the profession, whose obituaries will make even those readers who had assumed they had died long ago sigh at their youthful beauty and long to go backstage to express their belated appreciation. Zinnia had been born into show business, to a variety act called The Two Herberts who, while not entirely responsible for the death of music hall, were certainly in at its demise. Zinnia herself had made her début at the age of three, at the Hackney Empire, singing 'I've Never Seen A Straight Banana'. In fact, as it was wartime, she had never seen a banana at all.

She might have guessed, she thought in the taxi, that any production staged at a venue with such an unpleasant name, recalling ancient cruelties, would be dire. The Pillory Theatre was the converted billiard room of an old gin palace, and specialized in previously unperformed, and often never seen again, works by young playwrights. Zinnia and Alfred had perched uncomfortably on the edge of the avant-garde, on an itchy banquette which was a superannuated bus seat blobbed with polished strings of chewing gum, and scarred by cigarette burns that sighed puffs of dust at every shift of haunch and hip. A fellow critic acknowledged Zinnia and

Alfred with a languid wave, another rolled his eyes towards the kippered ceiling, and one or two people stared as if they thought they ought to recognize them, for Alfred, with his beard, green silk scarf, fedora and unlit cigar, cut as theatrical a figure as Zinnia in her russet fur, sniffing a scented handkerchief as if it were an orange stuffed with cloves or a nosegay wafted by a disdainful spectator at a historical scene of public humiliation. The rank air was noisy with the ripping of ringpulls and the crackle of discarded plastic cups that had held wine. Zinnia looked at the programme of *Istambull* and groaned.

'You didn't remind me. I can't stand two-handers. I'm always hoping for a knock on the door or for somebody to come jaunting in through the french windows.'

No scenery and not a french window in sight, not even a telephone to relieve the tedium; it was quite obviously not going to be her sort of play, and then a cat-o-nine tails of blond braids whipped her face and red wine splashed over her ankles as latecomers barged past with a surly demand of 'Scuse me'.

'I'm afraid I can't. You are inexcusable,' Zinnia told them, adding to Alfred, 'do you remember the days when people said, "Excuse me, *please*"?'

'You are at your most *grande dame* tonight. I love it. Marry me,' he whispered into her hair.

'Well, they might at least do the perpetrators of this sorry

195

entertainment the courtesy of arriving on time, particularly as it started twenty-two minutes late. Besides, I'm married.'

Afterwards, outside on the pavement, wrinkling her nose at her coat sleeve, Zinnia said, 'I feel as if I've spent the evening in an old chip pan, or in the dustbag of a Hoover that hasn't been emptied for years. And I'm sure several vertebrae have fused.'

'You might have woken me,' Alfred complained. 'You know I always sleep through the first act, and as there was no interval ... presumbly to prevent any escape at half time. I give the director credit for that at least. Did you manage to get your head down at all?'

'Only forty winks right at the end. Why can't young people speak any more? That dreary sub-dialect they all use – I mean *yews*. They're all at it, actors, weather girls, broadcasters. And have shampoos and dry cleaners gone out of fashion?'

'Yoo hoo, Dolly!'

A middle-aged woman was waving at them from across the street, calling the name of a character Zinnia had played in a recent television sitcom, one of the dotty next-door-neighbour parts which casting directors had made rather her forté.

'Yoo hoo yourself!' Zinnia responded, waggling a zany little wave, with a daffy smile, through a gap in the traffic.

'Let's get out of here,' she said. 'Where would you like to eat? *I'm* taking *you*, as you treated me to that delightful show. Such a glamorous life you lead, my dear.'

'Don't be silly, *I* invited *you*. What do you feel like eating? I don't know about you, but I'd just like a bowl of noodles.'

Zinnia slipped her arm through his, remembering with affection how this big, powerful, rich man had always sought comfort from food served in round, peasant or nursery shapes – a plate of pasta, a bowl of soup, a pot of tea, a dish of lentils – and how he was not above tucking a napkin under his chin on occasion, and how his chopsticks would glean the last grains of rice from a succession of ceramic lotus leaves; and a whiff of his *eau de toilette* brought a pang of regret.

'Let's find you some noodles, then. How about the Golden Dragon over there?'

'Or you could just come home with me, and I'll bring you something delicious on a tray.'

It was as much the impossibility of superimposing her present-day self on Alfred's memory of her as the thought of her husband Norman at home that made Zinnia pull Alfred briskly to the restaurant. They both had children older than most of the Pillory audience, she a daughter by her first marriage and two granddaughters, Alfred two sons and three grandchildren, and Norman's son's girlfriend was expecting a baby. Zinnia was more excited than Norman by the news; she adored babies and shopping for them. Norman was grumpy about becoming a grandfather, although he was well of an age for such an event. Zinnia felt a frisson of desire, a flattered flutter, at Alfred's suggestion. But at her age. And she had spent so many years atoning for her own successes and polishing Norman's fallen star that she had lost all sense of herself as desirable. Norman Bannerman had been a big name in television drama in the Seventies and now, when there was such a dearth of new plays on the small screen, he was all but forgotten.

'I wonder if old Norm's plays have stood the test of time?' mused Alfred, painting a little pancake with plum jam. 'Do you think they'd hold water now?'

'Of course they would! They're plays, not sponges or colanders! If you take that away from Norman, you leave him with nothing, As a matter of fact, he's working on a stage play now, and I'm sure it's going to be wonderful. You have a noodle in your beard.' Zinnia took a sip of jasmine tea from a tiny cup of scalding porcelain emblazoned with a dragon.

'I don't know – I'm afraid they might have dated badly. Poor Norman,' Alfred persisted.

'Noodle. Remove it, please.'

Zinnia was starting to feel a remembered irritation.

'You'll have to fill me in on tonight's débâcle,' Alfred

went on. 'I don't suppose you thought to make any notes, did you?'

Habit made her apologize.

'Come home with me. You can fax Norm to say you won't be back.' He flipped the last pancake on to her plate.

'Just along there on the right, please,' Zinnia told the taxi driver. 'Past the big tree.'

Ingram Road was a curve of white stuccoed terrace houses, like a thousand London streets, with nothing taller than a slender eucalypt, a magnolia or an occasional misshapen pollarded lime in its walled front gardens, but there was one Olympic plane tree growing out of the pavement, whose shadows dappled the houses on either side and across the road with light and shade like the patches on its great trunk. The plane's bare branches hung with shrivelled fruits splashed moonlight over Zinnia as she stepped out and the taxi's running motor set off a scolding car alarm. She hurried into the house before an irate neighbour could identify her as the culprit, without asking for the receipt which Norman would demand in the morning. A paper lantern shone in the front room of the new young couple next door. It was not Joel and Maxine's fault that they knew nothing of the history of Ingram Road, or that to the older residents Number Eighteen, where they had moved so cheerfully and noisily with a hired van and a gang of friends helping, would always be the house where widowed Jim Bacon had been barbecued on his late wife's electric blanket. Joel and Maxine had a little silver cat called Mignonette, who wore a pearlized flea collar that was luminous in the dark.

Upstairs Norman switched off his bedside lamp and lay resenting the discreet clatter of Zinnia washing up his supper things. At last he heard the stairs creak, then the sound of the bathroom shower and the whine of the hair dryer. She came noiselessly into the bedroom on velvet mules, bathed the dressing table in a kindly apricot glow and sat down to brush her hair. He thought she looked like a B-movie actress playing a film star. There ought to be lightbulbs round the mirror reflecting that slithery kimono slipping off one shoulder, he decided, the sleeve falling back up her arm as her hair leaped to the bristles of her silver brush. A ritual hundred strokes for the head that had long ago lost its golden lustre. Norman blacked out several of his imaginary lightbulbs, swept aside the pots of theatrical unguents and goo to make room for a bottle of gin, and tacked a broken star to her dressing-room door. This was a dame on the skids. Box-office poison. Then, in embittered inspiration, he had her peel off her eyelashes and pull off her wig to reveal the bald, clichéd head of a drag queen.

'Well, well, well, if it isn't Mrs Norman Maine! Tell me, my dear, how went the show tonight?'

Zinnia's gasp at his voice, and the clashing of glass bottles on the glass-topped dressing table as she dropped her brush, gave Norman a visceral wriggle of pleasure.

'Darling! I hope I didn't wake you. I was trying to be so quiet.'

'I heard you taking a no doubt much-needed shower.'

'You're not kidding! I felt absolutely soiled — contaminated.'

Embarrassment as fine as a cloud of powder from a powderpuff drifted across the room as Zinnia, realizing the implications of this exchange, unscrewed a jar of face cream. Norman was at his most dangerous in his *A Star is Born* mode. If only his parents hadn't called him Norman he might not identify so with the leading man of the film whose own star fell as his wife's rose.

'So, apart from that, how did you enjoy the play, Mrs Lincoln?'

'It was filthy. The theatre was filthy, and the play was filthy. Self-indulgent, illiterate, pathetically boorish. So depressing, it's as if Shakespeare, Chekhov, Ibsen, Beckett, you of course, or any of the great dramatists had never lived …'

Zinnia worried that she should have placed Norman higher in this pantheon, perhaps between Shakespeare and Chekhov, but all he needed to know was the play had been rubbish, and relieved, he said, 'Sorry you had a rotten evening, but I did warn you, didn't I?'

'You did,' she said ruefully and gratefully. 'I should have listened. I thought it might be a lark, but it turned out to be' — she thought of the Chinese restaurant — 'a dead duck.'

The smell of the cream which Zinnia was smoothing into her arched throat brought Norman a memory of lying in his mother's bed, a sick child propped up on her pillows, watching her rubbing in Pond's Vanishing Cream. It had never worked though, he reflected. Mother was with them still. He decided to visit her the following afternoon. It would beat another long day in the garden chewing the lonely cud of nonentity, while Zinnia was off recording voice-overs for washing-up liquid commercials, and then watching television with his unfinished play dozing fretfully like an untended baby on his desk.

Zinnia got into bed and reached for his hand beneath the covers. Deliberately mistaking her intention, for neither could remember the last time anything more than a homely hug had passed between them, Norman, a dog with the bone of jealousy clamped in his teeth, said, 'Do you mind awfully, old girl? Sorry to let you down, but I'm feeling somewhat queasy. That casserole you left me must have been a bit off. Been in the freezer too long, I guess. Nothing to worry about, I'm sure — I hardly touched it. Chucked it in the bin as soon as I realized. Blimey, Zin, you've been on the garlic, haven't you? Hope your chum was too, for his sake. Or should I say saké? I've seen that gin bottle in your dressing room. You'd better get a grip on yourself, people are starting to talk.'

Bewildered and hurt, flushing in the smooth nightdress that suddenly irritated her skin, Zinnia asked, 'What on earth do you mean?' But Norman had rolled over into contented sleep. She wished with all her heart, with her clenched fists and tears leaking into her lavender-scented pillow, that she was in Alfred's kelim-covered bed in his dark, frankincense-and-myrrh-fragrant mansion flat. Alfred's antecedents had sailed from Smyrna. His grandfather had opened the family carpet business in the Burlington Arcade and his uncles and brothers were importers of dried fruits and nuts, and dealers in works of art and sweet heavy wines, otto of roses, orris root and amber. Zinnia pictured heaps of dates and figs, salted almonds, cashews, pistachios, halva, Turkish delight sleeted with soft sugar, frosted glacé bonbons, glowing embroideries and sheer bolts of silken colour. While Alfred lay in damask sheets beneath exiled textiles, the personification of the romantic Levant, Norman the Nebbish snored softly beside her in striped pyjamas buttoned to the neck with his breath giving little snickers, as if he were making jokes at somebody's expense in his dreams. If only she had married Alfred when they had first met, but she hadn't, and they had both married, and divorced, other people. Then, when she was single again, and her beloved daughter Nerissa away at university, she had fallen for Norman's lanky, vulnerable charm. Zinnia had forgiven and forgiven Norman for his cruelty, because she knew it stemmed from his own pain, but she felt unable to bear much more of his malice. Yet, even now, if bitter, going-to-seed Norman were to turn to her, she would take him in her arms.

In the morning, Norman found himself alone in bed, vaguely aware of a breakfast tray on his bedside table, of gilded strands in the marmalade and rainbows playing about the facets of the crystal jar, and lay half-dozing. His thoughts were tender, vulnerable things, green walnuts, soft-shell crabs on a damp seashore, a violet snail reflected in a pavement after rain, unfledged birds in pink and mauve, the fuzzy green almond buds of the magnolia, little boys. Norman wrestled languorously with his conscience, hardly breaking sweat, knowing he could lick it with one hand tied behind his back; he overpowered it and flung it into a pathetic whimpering heap beside the bed. He reached for the forbidden bookshelf in his memory and took down a faded volume with a picture of schoolboys on its torn cover, riffling through the specked pages until he found his place. What Norman liked best was the beating of boys, preferably in some raffish educational establishment on the south coast, but what he could never determine was whether he wanted to be Old Seedy, the gowned and mortar-boarded avenger, or one of Seedy's devil-may-care but ultimately chastised and chastened young tormenters. The swells and eddies of desire, the sucking surf, the quivering rod, the crashing waves outside the mullioned windows, the breakfast tray flying, caught by a guilty elbow as his wife, with misplaced levity, popped her turbanned head round the door to enquire brightly, 'Can I do you now, sir?'

In a second she was on her knees, scrabbling among the spilled breakfast things, apologizing,

'I'm so sorry, I thought you'd have finished by now. I'll get you some fresh tea and toast as soon as I've mopped this lot up. Entirely my fault.'

'For God's sake, woman. You're not in *ITMA* now. You always have to be on, don't you?'

'What do you mean, *on*? And you know I'm not old enough to have been in *ITMA*. It was supposed to be a joke.'

She sat back on her heels to face him.

'*On*. You of all people should know what *on* means. On stage. On camera. Performing. Playing to the gallery. You can't even do a bit of housework without getting yourself up like Mrs Miniver in a pinny or Lucille Ball prancing around with a feather duster, can you?'

Zinnia's hand flew to her scarf-wrapped head, she glanced

205

down at her striped matelot top, toreador pants and ballet slippers, and a blush crept up her neck and burned her face.

'I just bunged on the first things that came to hand, to do a few chores.'

'Forget the breakfast, I don't feel up to it anyway. Just get me some Pepto-Bismol and a glass of water. You'll be pleased to know that by barging in like that you've completely broken my train of thought and probably destroyed my play. I hope you're satisfied.'

Zinnia stared at him in horror, a person from Porlock who had pranced roughshod in ballet shoes through her husband's dreams, opening her mouth to beg forgiveness for something that could never be put right, but before she could speak Norman went on, 'Isn't it time you were off to do your washing-up commercial? Don't let me keep you. Your public awaits, and you're dressed for the part. "These are the dreams of an everyday housewife ..."' he sang.

At the sneer in his voice, Zinnia, her lip quivering, said, 'Funnily enough, when I was putting out the rubbish I didn't see any sign of that casserole you said you threw away. *You* used to do that once, remember? Put the garbage out on dustbin day.'

'Perhaps it wasn't food poisoning after all. Could be a recurrence of my old complaint, chronic Zinniaphobia. Anyhow, don't bother about leaving me lunch, I'm going out, as I expect you've forgotten, but I can't expect a star of stage, screen and the kitchen sink to remember the mechanics of my dull life, can I?'

'I hadn't forgotten, as you didn't tell me. Look, Norman, I had hoped that we could make a fresh start this morning, but I see I was wrong. I'm sorry I went to the theatre with Alfred last night. It was a mistake. But it was all perfectly innocent, I assure you. Don't humiliate me by pretending to think otherwise. That's what all this is about, isn't it? You're jealous because I saw Alfred.'

'You flatter yourself, duckie.'

When Norman stumped off to the bathroom, Zinnia caught sight of herself in the mirror and saw that she looked very silly indeed. She wanted to telephone Nerissa, but it had never been her way to whinge. She blew her nose and was wiping her eyes when Norman came back into the bedroom with his bare chest looking its age in the morning sunshine. The ache of affection she felt then was obliterated when he said, 'Chin up, Mrs Miniver. Smile though your heart is breaking, laugh, clown, laugh, and all that crap. Even when the darkest cloud is in the sky, you musn't sigh and you mustn't – attagirl, big blow now, troupe away, my brave little trouper, the show must go on.'

Zinnia screamed at him, 'This is not a movie – it's our lives! You're not Norman Maine! At least Norman Maine had the decency to walk out to sea and look like James

Mason! You know who you are? Norma Desmond! That's who you are, Norma Desmond!'

'That makes you a dead monkey then. And at least Judy Garland had the grace to overdose.'

Ingram Road was where the boys of St Joseph's School came to smoke and eat takeaways in their breaks, and the residents often slipped on greasy chicken bones. As he left the house, Norman came upon old Father Coyle, a shrunken praying mantis who occupied a grace-and-favour apartment in the attic of the Palladian school building, prodding with his stick a vinegary chip paper that had adhered to the trunk of the plane tree. Father Coyle, in his little black suit and biretta that was too large for his head, often took his constitutional along Ingram Road, hoping to catch out truanting pupils, even though he was too frail now to do more than shake his stick at them.

'Not long till Easter now, Father,' Norman remarked encouragingly.

'Is that so, so?' replied Father Coyle.

Norman went on his way, in real life, in a blue morning pouring through the spreading, arching, gracefully trailing twigs of the tree, where Old Seedy's gown was a grubby rag stuffed away somewhere and forgotten, and a pair of passing schoolboys in their untucked shirts and black blazers attracted neither a thought nor a glance. The daytime

Norman, who would sicken at the notion of striking a child, set off on his journey to visit his mother.

Maria Bannerman lived in sheltered accommodation in West Kensington. She had had to sell Norman's birthright, the family home, to afford her self-contained flatlet in Glebe Park, a purpose-built block with a resident warden on the premises in case of emergencies. Norman's father, who had died at ninety in full possession of his faculties, had owned a small engineering works which had specialized in making tin openers. The recession had almost put him out of business and the ringpull revolution, particularly in the petfood industry, would have bankrupted him had he not had the vision to diversify into shackles, leg-irons and handcuffs for home use and export to select regimes abroad, and electric prods that were licensed to teach cattle a lesson but destined to burn smoother flesh as well. The company, Bannerman Aluminium & Steel (GB) had been sold, at a loss, on Norman's father's death so, as Zinnia had remarked, Norman was spared making any major Shavian or Ibsonian decisions about his inheritance. He was glad to be shot of the firm and his father's disappointment that it was never Bannerman & Son. He had hated working there in the holidays, fearing the sharp, ribald apprentices and the cynical, laconic foreman, but what a success his first television play *Pigs and Spigots* had been, set on the shopfloor, with cradles and ladles of molten steel and dialogue that had jammed the switchboard with protests.

His mother was ninety-two and fit as a flea, although, with her bright eyes magnified by the spectacles clamped to her beak and fuzz of white hair, she looked, to Norman, like a fledgling in a flowered overall. He found her pegging washing on to the communal lines in the garden behind the flats. Her next-door neighbour Jack Bedwell, whose television could be heard shouting a racing commentary through his closed window, was holding a basket of wet clothes, which contained, to Norman's distaste, several items of his mother's underwear.

'Norman! What a lovely surprise! I hope this doesn't mean you won't be coming at Easter?' she added anxiously.

'No mother. I just felt like coming to see you. We'll all be there at Easter, three-line whip, eh?'

He knew family visits on the prescribed occasions were vital to the residents' prestige.

'Zinnia's not with you today then, son?'

Maria looked hopefully down the path, through borders of forsythia at its yellow apotheosis, with the green about to take over.

'Sorry. I did ask her, but you know how it is with these famous actresses ...'

'We was just talking about you,' put in Jack, passing Maria a pair of bloomers. 'I was only saying to your mum,

210

when's your Norman going to get the old BBC to put on some of his plays again? With all the old rubbish and repeats they have on nowadays, they can't be any worse than them, can they? You want to have a word. It's all cops and crime and hospitals, where's the entertainment in that? Get enough of that as it is, thank you very much. Old Elsie had 'er pension snatched last week, only a young kid, he was. I'd chop off their hands if it was up to me. I'd do it myself.'

'Shall we go in, Mother, if you've finished?' Norman took the plastic basket from the old man.

'Used to be a really pleasant area round here in the old days,' Jack went on. 'Now it's liquorice allsorts. Remember, Maria, when we had the old muffin man come round, and the milkman with his horse and cart and the cats' meat man ...'

'The cats' meat man!' exclaimed Maria, and the two old people stared mistily into the distance, as if the cats' meat man would descend from the clouds to save them all.

In his mother's flat Norman drank tea from a cup that tasted of bleach. The muffin man, he thought, that's pushing it a bit, and pictured a nursery-rhyme figure in striped stockings, with a bell and a tray round his neck, but he had to sympathize just a little with the old people, who felt like aliens in their childhood landscape, which had changed out of all recognition.

'When you live on your own', his mother explained, not for the first time, when he complained of the taste of bleach in his cup, 'you can't afford to let things slide, you've got to keep everything up to scratch. Of course, Shirley, my home help, comes in, as you know, but she's from the criminal classes, bless her. One of those big families of the criminal aristocracy. I suppose, being brought up to prison and hospitals from an early age, it was natural that she should be drawn to disinfectant, even if she isn't as thorough as I'd like. She doesn't need to work, you know, her husband's got a shop off the market, specializes in reproduction antiques and chandeliers, all the genuine article. Shirley was a nursing auxiliary for a while and then she cleaned the police canteen, but that didn't suit her either. Her home's a little palace from what she tells me, a regular Aladdin's cave. More tea, son? A piece of cream cake? It's only just past its sell-by, Shirley got it for me.'

As Norman sipped and nodded, his alter ego, Larry Parnes blacked up for the Jolson Story, detached itself from his body and fell to its knees, clasping Maria round the waist in its white-gloved hands and burying its face in her flowered lap. Don't you know me, Mammy? I'm your little baby!

Norman departed uncomforted, leaving his mother in her few square feet of life, scouring the stainless-steel sink, keeping things up to scratch. Exhausted and irritable after the long journey home by tube and bus in the rush hour, he breathed the air of Ingram Road with relief, noting the song of a blackbird on a satellite dish and daffodils in the gardens. Maxine from next door was coaxing the little cat Mignonette down from the lowest branch of the plane tree.

'Beautiful evening', said Norman. 'There's a real hint of spring in the air at last.'

'Yeah, I know. Everything coming into bud, and the blossom out.' Maxine patted the tree trunk, with the cat over her shoulder in its collar silvered with the glimmering early evening light.

'Dear old tree,' she said. 'I'm going to miss it.'

'What do you mean, miss it? You're not moving again already, are you?'

She was a pretty girl, her arms poignant in the sleeves of her boyfriend's pink polo shirt.

'Oh no. It's just our insurance company. They say it's got to come down. I'm really, really sad, because I'm very much a tree person, very into trees, but they won't insure us unless it comes down, because of the roots. In case they cause problems in the future. Ouch, Mignonette, you're scratching me. I'd better go in.'

She backed away, clutching the struggling cat.

'No, wait! You can't just land a bombshell like that and walk away!'

Norman grabbed her arm, the cat leaped away, and Joel

213

appeared, with a can of Coke in his hand, saying, 'Everything all right, Maxie? Take your hand off her arm. What do you think you're doing? I'll have you for assault if you don't watch out.'

'Is it true, what she just said, about the tree?'

''Fraid so, mate. Shame, but there you go.'

'But you can't just do that! You can't just move in like vandals and chop down mature trees to suit yourselves. There are laws about that sort of thing. It's ridiculous. We'll see what the Council has to say about it. I'll get a preservation order if necessary.'

'Too late, mate. The Council has given its consent. It can't afford to take on the insurance company in the courts, so it's caved in under the threat of litigation. What's called market forces, old chap.'

'No it isn't, it's called hooliganism!' said Norman. 'I don't believe I'm hearing this. Tell me I'm dreaming, somebody. Are you two aware that the paid thugs of cable television have destroyed the roots of thousands of trees all over London so that their pornography can be piped into the homes of people like you? Are you?'

'Let's go in, Joel,' said Maxine.

'Hang on.' Joel shrugged her off. 'Nobody talks to me like that. I've a good mind to kick his head in.'

'Just try it, punk.' Norman thrust a clenched fist under Joel's chin. 'Come on, I dare you.'

'Oh, leave him, Joel, he's not worth it. He's just a twisted old loony.'

'Old loony, am I?' Norman swung a punch, which Joel sidestepped.

'Zinnia!' Norman yelled, with tears of rage in his eyes, 'Zinnia! Where are you, you stupid cow? Come and give me a bit of support for once in your life, damn you!'

He turned back to Maxine and Joel.

'I thought you young people were all about saving the planet? What about the environment you're all so keen on? What about the Newbury bypass protesters, then? Young people, and old, risking life and limb to try to save those trees, living in tunnels, yes, and the opponents of the export of live veal calves who have lain down their very lives for their principles, and you stand there calmly telling me that you have arranged the murder of the oldest, noblest, most majestic tree in this street. Old Jim and Edith Bacon must be turning in their graves! You ought to be ashamed of yourselves. Is this the sort of world you want for your children? Don't you walk away from me! Come back here!'

Norman kicked their gate, hurting his foot on wrought iron.

'Goths and Visigoths! Barbarians! Veal-eating, Coke-swilling pigs, I hope you die of mad cow disease!' he shouted at their slammed front door.

Where the hell was Zinnia when he needed her? There

was no note, no sign of any supper. Not knowing what to do with himself, Norman poured a glass of whisky and went into his study. He saw at once that the pages of his play had been disturbed, but he was in such turbulence himself, agitating his drink into a whirlpool that spiralled out of the glass and splashed everything in its radius, that the violation of his work scarcely registered. As the confrontation replayed in his mind, he became aware of faces watching it from neighbouring windows. He put down his glass and went out again, to ring the doorbell of the Patels who lived opposite.

After Norman had left the house that morning, Zinnia had not known what to do with herself. She had worked hard all her life, she had paid her dues. Surely she was entitled to enjoy what success she had without Norman spoiling everything and making a nonsense of her life? Yes, she was a trouper. Was that something to be mocked and sneered at? Why could he not just let her *be*, without judging her every action like some sarcastic schoolmaster or a vicious director humiliating her in front of the rest of the cast and making her forget her lines? She had a recurrent nightmare now, of being late for the theatre and running and running along endless backstage corridors, through doors which opened into surreal dressing rooms, until at last she stood on the stage in tears, trying to force her voice through locked lips above the babel of the audience. But no sound would come, and when she looked down at herself, she was naked or dressed in a clown's costume. She remembered how Norman, on his way out, had asked, 'Anything in the post?'

'Nothing to write home about', she had replied, concealing the letter inviting her to open the fête at their local hospice.

At a loss, in the kitchen, she stared at the vermicelli of a hydroponic hyacinth on the windowsill and saw that overnight two strawberries left on a plate had bloated and their seeds turned black like the bristles in a drunk's bruised red face. She drifted into Norman's study with the feather duster still in her hand. The heart of the Evil Empire, she thought. She was forbidden to touch Norman's desk, but this morning, with the sun casting a tracery of plane tree twigs and bobbles over the word processor, the papers, books and writer's paraphernalia and toys, and glinting on the gold pen Norman's dad had left him, the pen that Norman had to use for all his 'real', his creative, work, Zinnia picked up the manuscript of Norman's unfinished play, *The Last Sand Dance*.

Act I, Scene i. A seedy theatre somewhere in the provinces. The stage is lightly sprinkled with sand. Enter stage left shuffling, two sad old vaudevilleans, male and female, in striped blazers and flannels, bent stiffly at the waist and waving straw boaters and clutching canes. Turning to the sparse audience of comatose pensioners, *he* sings in a cracked cockney voice,

> 'When you wore a turnip,
> A big yellow turnip,
> And I wore a big red nose …'

while *she* executes a grim little dance. Onstage costume change …

Zinnia sank back into Norman's chair. Her legs were weak and tingling, the little hairs on the back of her neck and arms standing on end. 'You bastard! How could you do this to us?' He had dug up her dead parents and was killing them again with his pen. She read on, clammy in her matelot top, the horripilant pages trembling in her hand.

Onstage costume change. The straw boaters are sent whizzing into the wings, and Egyptian robes and red fezes with black tassels thrown unceremoniously on. The aged pair catch them clumsily and struggle into them over their blazers, etc. They break into a grotesque sand dance, à la Wilson, Keppel (Kepple?) and Betty. Tot runs on, stage left, tripping cutely over her too-long Egyptian robe, holding her fez on with one hand and staggering under the weight of a giant papier-maché banana. Sings, 'I've Never Seen a Straight Banana' …

'Wakey, Wa-key!! Hey, you down there with the banana!'

At the disembodied voice of Billy Cotton, the trio cower and crouch like victims of an air raid as an enormous balloon with the spectacled features of the great bandleader floats down from the gods, and his signature tune blares out, Dah, dada dah dah dah, Somebody Stole My Gal …

Zinnia was shaking, and nauseous at the knowledge of her own innocent collaboration in this parading of her family to public scorn. It was she who had told Norman how the Two Herberts had been turned away from their audition for the Billy Cotton Band Show on the wireless and how it had broken The Two Herberts' hearts. 'Boater? What boater?' she heard her father's voice in memory, 'I thought you said put on your bloater!' He had a large fish on his head.

Her eye caught the glitter of Norman's fountain pen. The murder weapon. Although she could hardly bear to touch it, she picked it up, feeling the weight of its machine-turned gold in her hand. A pen bought with the proceeds from manufacturing instruments of torture. So that is what they mean by the banality of evil, she thought. Its agents are the jovial grandpa finding a sixpence behind a grandchild's ear, the benevolent boss with a pen clipped to his clean overall pocket as he jokes with his employees on the shop floor, the Rotarian adding an afterthought to his speech at the charity dinner.

'Your play stinks, Norman,' she said aloud. 'It stinks to high heaven. The only place bad enough to stage it is the Pillory Theatre.'

Zinnia threw the pen to the floor and stamped on it, but it would not break. It rolled from her ballet pump, hard and inviolate. She tried to grind it into the carpet. The cap came off, but still the pen was unharmed. She tried once more and failed, and then she picked up the shiny barrel. It was bleeding a little blue ink from the nib and had caught a piece of fluff, like a feather in a crossed beak. Zinnia opened the window and flung the pen and its cap as hard as she could. She heard them bounce off next door's dustbin. Then she telephoned her daughter.

'Nerissa, I have nourished a viper in my bosom.'

Much later that night the telephone rang again in Nerissa's house. Nerissa's husband picked it up.

'Stephen?' said Norman's voice. 'I don't suppose you have any idea of where my wife might be? She seems to have disappeared and I'm getting a bit worried. It isn't like her.'

'She's here, if it's any of your concern,' said Norman's step-son-in-law, and put down the phone.

✳   ✳   ✳

A fortnight or so after Easter, Zinnia's taxi driver stopped his cab at the corner of Ingram Road.

'I can't get through. Seems to be some sort of disturbance going on down there, or an accident. Looks like they've got the emergency services out.'

'Oh, I do hope it isn't anything dreadful! Can you wait for me here then? I'll be as quick as I can, I've just got to pick up a few things. Oh dear, there seem to be lots of people and the police!'

It flashed through her mind that Norman had killed himself, but reassuring herself that he was not Norman Maine, she hurried on. She could see spinning blue lights, flashing amber, yellow machinery, a heavy digger slewed across the road, a television camera crew, a banner strung across the street, a crowd holding hands around the trunk of the plane tree. They spilled over the pavement and into the road, shouting and singing 'We shall not be moved'. Zinnia stopped and looked up into the branches of the tree. There were huge black and white birds, vultures, huddled there, and she realized that they were boys from St Joseph's. At the top of the plane tree, as high as he could climb, stood Norman, arms outstretched, straddling two boughs.

His face, patterned by sun and shadows, was radiant, as if he were in his element, the air, at last, or he was an ancient tree deity returned to redeem the world of men. Below him, his people waved broken branches and twigs and sang hosannas. Tears were streaming down Zinnia's face. Everybody was there, all the neighbours, the Patels, the Smiths, the Peacocks, the Patterson-Dixes who spoke only Esperanto, Joel scuffling with somebody, that family of Exclusive Brethren who never spoke to anybody, and now, unbelievably, the boys were hauling old Father Coyle up in a hoist, with his skinny black silk ankles poking out like sticks and everybody cheering him.

A television reporter had made it almost up to Norman, who shouted down into the furry boom they call a dead rat, 'We are the people of Ingram Road, England and we had not spoken yet! But today now we have found our collective voice, and we are saying loud and clear, for all the world's media to hear, "Hands off our tree!" This is the will of the people and the people will be heard! The mighty plane tree shall not fall! There will be no chainsaw massacre here today or any other day!'

The wind ruffled his hair and billowed his white shirt, cleansing him of old familial shame and failure and recent guilts. He could hear, lower down, the buzzing of a saw, a policeman shouting, and he was aware of the boys scrambling and swinging from the branches like monkeys in their black blazers. As he caught the quavering benediction of Father Coyle through the swaying bunches of twigs, withered fruits and new baby growth, it came to him that all he had needed, all along, was an audience to make him whole again. Far beneath his triumphant feet, Old Seedy was cut to pieces by the teeth of the saw and sent flying in fragments of dry dead wood.

The crowd was swelling with the red-blazered girls of the comprehensive and latterday punks and hippies and eco-warriors with their dogs. Norman heard faint chimes of an ice-cream van over the din, and he almost lost his grip and his footing as he thought he saw Zinnia's distinctive tiny scarlet-tipped head above her foreshortened daffodil-yellow jacket, ducking into a black cab parked at the corner. It happened so quickly, and she was lost to sight so fast, in the blink of an eye, in the whisk of the tail of a rat leaping aboard a ship bound for the Gulf of Izmir before the tide turned.

'Read Mackay for her ability to describe murky subject matter with all the sensual splendour of a romantic poet'
Esther Brooks, *Time Out*

'A strangely beguiling mix of lunacy, anguish, and tenderness, observed in lucid, frugal prose...'
New York Times Book Review

'Her prose is flawlessly seductive and comic, confidently witty and sensual'
Julie Myerson, *Independent on Sunday*

'Sharp and original, Shena Mackay excels in transforming the mundane into the grotesque'
Literary Review

V

VINTAGE

Shena Mackay

A BOWL OF CHERRIES

'A splendid novel; poetic, witty and thoroughly interesting'
Iris Murdoch

'Macabre and fearless... she writes extremely well and it's a
joy to read her, whatever happens'
Financial Times

'Shena Mackay has the rare knack of making the ordinary
seem foreign and the improbable plausible through exertion
of sheer charm... More please'
Sunday Times

'Ms Mackay...possesses such an incisive comic gift, and
such a canny eye for the absurd, that her book, a treat
throughout, is frequently belly-laugh funny... a lovely book,
entertaining, insightful and, in the end, deeply satisfying'
New York Times Book Review

V

VINTAGE